**and other
Stories and Poems**

ISBN 0 905223 23 3

The publishers acknowledge the generous assistance
of the Arts Council in the publication of this book.

Cover design Hugh Donoghue
Typesetting Redsetter Ltd.
Printed by Cahill & Co. Ltd.
Published by Arlen House Ltd.,
2 Strand Road, Baldoyle, Dublin 13.

A DREAM
RECURRING

and other
Stories and Poems

Maxwell House Winners 2

ARLEN
HOUSE

IVY BANNISTER, born in New York in 1951, has been living in Ireland since 1970. A graduate of Trinity College, Dublin, her poems have been published in *The Irish Press* and *The Cork Examiner*. She is married and has one child.

PATRICIA BOYNE was born in Dublin and attended University College there. She was principal of a Dublin secretarial college for many years and since her retirement has been devoting more time to writing. A widow for many years she admits to being '70 plus'.

MARY DONOVAN was born in Dublin in 1953 but spent most of her childhood in County Tipperary. Qualified as a primary teacher in 1972, she worked in Israel and in Portugal and is now a teacher in a North County Dublin school. She has had stories published in *The Irish Press New Irish Writing*.

HONOR DUFF was born in Dublin in 1938. Her work has been published in various journals and broadcast on RTE Radio. Fluent in French and Spanish she has worked as a translator in Ireland and has taught English in Spain. Widowed, with one daughter, she works with a Dublin newspaper.

CARLA GOLDBERG, born in India in 1943, lived in Cheshire, England until she went to Dublin to read medicine at University College in 1962. Apart from short working visits to Spain, Canada and England she has lived in Dublin ever since. She is married and has one daughter. Her stories have previously been published in *The Irish Press*.

MARIE HURLEY was born in Charleville, Co. Cork in 1948. She spent four years at Limerick School of Art before going to Nairobi, Kenya, for a year. She taught briefly at a Secondary School in County Cork and now spends her time 'riding horses, tending cows and contemplating the countryside'.

RITA KELLY was born in Ballinasloe, County Galway in 1953. Since 1972 she has been living with her husband in an old Lock House, inaccessible except by boat, on the river Barrow near Carlow. Editor of *Eigse Carlow* a bi-lingual arts review, her work has been published both in Irish and in English in various journals including *The Irish Press, New Irish*

Writing, Comhar, Feasta, The Literary Review (Edinburgh) and has been broadcast on RTE Radio. She won *The Irish Times*/Merriman Poetry Award in 1975 and the Listowel Writers Week Award for humorous essay in 1976. She was recently awarded the Seán Ó Ríordáin Memorial Award at the Oireachtas.

JOYCE McGREEVY STAFFORD, winner of the poetry section, was born in Arizona, USA in 1955 but has lived in Ireland since she was thirteen. Educated in Limerick she is at present a student at University College, Galway. Married and now living in Galway, she has had stories and poetry published and is editor of *Voices*, an outlet for student writing at UCG.

SHEELAGH MORRIS, prize-winner in the story section, was born in Dublin in 1939. A night student at University College, Dublin before her children were born, she returned as a full time 'mature' student when they started school. At present she is a part-time lecturer in Sociology in two Dublin colleges. She is married and has two sons.

ELIZABETH A. O'BRIEN was born in Derry, Northern Ireland in 1959. As a young child she lived in Malta, returning to Derry when she was 10 years old. She spent a year at the University College of Wales at Aberystwyth before going to the Orkney Isles to work as a shell-fish processor. Returning to Derry in 1979, she became unemployed and joined the newly formed Derry Writers Workshop which published two issues of an Arts magazine. She is at present pursuing a career in accountancy.

Born in Callan, County Kilkenny in 1941 HARRIET O'CARROLL's first published story was amongst the winners in the first Maxwell House competition and was published in *The Wall Reader and Other Stories.* A practising physio-therapist she lives in Limerick with her husband and three children.

MARY REILLY was born in Luton, England in 1960 and has lived in Dublin since she was a child. A final-year Arts student at University College, Dublin, she has had Summer jobs 'washing dishes, serving beer, selling clothes and pricing books'.

MARY WALKIN, second prize winner in the story section was born in Bundoran, County Donegal in 1948. She subsequently lived and was educated in Cork, Castlebar, Dublin and Limerick. A graduate of the London College of Music (Speech & Drama) she now lives in Toronto, Canada with her husband and two sons. In 1979 she won the *Toronto Star* short story competition.

GABRIELLE WARNOCK was born in West Cork in 1947 and educated at Rochelle School in Cork. She has lived and travelled extensively in England and the United States and since 1977 has been living in Kinvara, County Galway with her husband and two sons. She has had two stories published in *The Irish Press New Irish Writing* and won second prize in the Listowel Writers Week Short Story Competition in 1980.

Contents

Preface *by Marie Mhac an tSaoi*

Preface

Máire Mhac an tSaoi

In 1978 Arlen House, The Women's Press, with the welcome encouragement and practical help of Maxwell House, held a competition for short stories written by women authors who had not previously been published. The resultant entries were of a remarkably high standard, and the best of them, after a long and careful appraisal by the judges, all of them writers of acknowledged stature and two of them women, were published in paperback format under the intriguingly ambiguous title of *The Wall Reader*, borrowed from the overall winner's entry. Encouraged by this success the promoters of the competition proceeded to a second, and those of the new entries adjudged best are now collected here and set before the public headed by that of the first-prize-winner, *A Dream Recurring*. It will be interesting to see whether they in their turn will meet the delighted welcome accorded to their predecessor. I am confident that they will at least make their mark, although they may have a somewhat harder struggle for attention now that the edge has been taken off the novelty of a literary competition confined to women only.

Be that as it may, it is surely a matter for careful consideration that over such a short period so much hitherto untapped talent should be found to exist among women, most, if not quite all, of whom are living in this country. The richness of the seam this competition has struck is in itself a most important justification for its continuance and for its continuance on its own terms. Theoretical objections to confining a literary competition to one sex only have already been ably met in the Preface to *The Wall Reader* by Eavan Boland, a judge on that occasion and again on this.

Briefly the case for the promoters can best be clarified by analogy: some injustices, such as the caste system and chattel slavery, are so deep-seated and enduring that they cannot be righted without the appearance of short-term and relatively innocuous unfairness, favouring the victims as against the privileged. Once it has been conceded that the lot of women authors falls in this category, the term discrimination no longer necessarily conveys a pejorative meaning. It takes on its more desirable sense and presupposes judgement, experience and mature reflection. The judges of this latest competition feel that the organisers have shown all three qualities and hope that they themselves will not be found wanting in them either. In one respect the scope of this round has been extended: it now includes poetry as well as prose, and indeed, for this writer at least, the most splendid revelation to emerge from the fascinating task of the judging was the prize-winning poem, *These Needles Through Our Own Lives Too Have Moved*, a truly remarkable instance of that communication across the barriers of time and space which many experienced in *The Wall Reader* and which the judges were to find again as we sifted this competition.

At this point let me make explicit my earlier reference to an ambiguity in the title *The Wall Reader*, an inspired ambiguity, let me add, such as is often the stuff of great poetry. I had thought before reading the story that the term referred to the sort of glazed showcase which used to be found outside the offices of all newspapers where the columns of the latest edition can be read by passers-by for free. I had recently seen wall newspapers in Russia and assumed that this was the idea behind the title, that these women had nailed up their appeal in some public place as Luther did his theses in Wittemburg, or as a Royal proclamation might be displayed on a village green. The misunderstanding proved tenacious of life and fertile in significance to an extent only partly dissipated by the reading of the short story itself. It still seems to me to epitomise the main function of this competition and of the Women's Press generally, that of bringing together people who in our sadly isolated contemporary life might never otherwise meet and enabling them to enjoy each other's companionship and to know each other better. To read the entries to this competition is to make friends. Women reading them will find companionship and support, men a broadening and enrichment of the imagination. Here it is the 'book' rather than the 'box' which constitutes the 'global village' and the comfort of a shared perception of events waits for us on the doorstep.

It is possibly a subjective impression that this second collection has a more sombre colouring than the first? I put down *The Wall Reader* with a sensation of altruism and optimism as realities and a comfortable belief that these were special and important factors in the world of women as such. Here any such feeling is entirely absent: frustration and cynicism are dominant — no hint of a happy ending. Even the high comedy of *Cherubim* has sinister undertones. Only the serenity of the prize-winning poem redeems the general gloom. How far is this the result of a random grouping? And if this is so and the phenomenon is entirely the product of coincidence can we not attach to it at least the importance of an omen? It may not be possible to see it as a symptom of the steadily worsening quality of daily life — and perhaps particularly of daily life as lived by women — but as the French say *tout aussi comme!* Signs and portents are not necessarily responsible to statistical analysis. The pious and the prudent take heed of the warning chance has vouchsafed them and move to remedy or avert the disaster. It would be *hubris* to act otherwise, and I do not think our society can afford this risk. The publishers and sponsors of this little book have made a practical and generous contribution towards righting at least one of the wrongs we, our society that is, labour under. For many of my generation for whom, daughters reacting against mothers who had been pillars of the women's suffrage movement and of the new state, the function of talent and intelligence in a woman seemed primarily biological, it is a revelation at once both disturbing and reassuring to meet work of this calibre so widely distributed. Surely this can be no mere spin-off of the survival of the species. Even if this were so — and the fact that these are all short pieces must be taken into account — should we complain? A by-product as sturdy as this has earned an independent welcome. As with the omen let us not delve too deeply, but be grateful for so much interest and pleasure, derived from and added to existence, simply and unaffectedly without further moralising or speculation.

Máire Mhac an tSaoi
Dublin, October 1980

A Dream Recurring

Sheelagh Morris

HE MARRIED in the autumn of 1956 but it was not until the early weeks of summer, twenty years later, that Mr. Wolff became aware that Mrs. Wolff was visibly crumbling. The rapid eviction of illusion, facilitated by the reality of marriage, had in general dulled his sensitivity to his wife's appearance and mental condition, but the visible breaking up of the physical edifice that he had married was alarming. This extraordinary situation was heightened by the fact that Mrs. Wolff herself seemed unaware of any problem.

Her fine parchment skin, so attractive to him in youth, had begun with the first heat of that perverse summer to lightly snow; by mid-July the flurry quickened until it seemed his home was covered in a fine cloud of skin droppings. He never asked the cause or suggested remedies. After one year of marriage and nineteen years of sharing a dwelling he did not often speak to Mrs. Wolff and certainly not upon a subject so personal as the deciduous nature of her skin.

It had been her skin which had attracted him in the dowdy limbo years that Ireland and Mr. Wolff passed through in the 'fifties. He was then thirty-five years old and had known no passion, pain nor even much quiet pleasure — a common animal to emerge from the repressed years of a bitter country turned in upon itself to pick spitefully at its sores. Unattractive physically, he had an image of himself; a man of letters, a wit, an arid intellectual living in cooler clearer airs, lending flesh to the role of owner/manager of his city bookshop. A Dublin personality not yet discovered but soon to flaunt and flash at the tables of the capital's elite. Those few tables to which he made it by default found him a bore and avoided encores.

It was his practice to eat lunch (which he had carefully prepared the night before in his Seapoint house where he lived alone and which was serviced by a daily) in the small room behind the shop. He ate quickly and alone, the one employee, a half-witted under-paid, under-educated product of a charity convent, sitting at the cash register in the semi-dark of the shop, lank hair over her eye, left hand, when not ringing the odd sale, in a permanent nose-picking position. Hers was not a glamorous life.

It was from such gloom that Mr. Wolff crept out one Monday lunchtime in June 1956. In packing his lunch the evening before he had overlooked his essential 'granny', as he called it, and, out of deference to his bowels, he stopped at a newly-opened fruit shop on the way to his daily perambulation of St. Stephen's Green. Inside was an Aladdin's cave of colour, smell and texture. Artistic cravings had piled, in pyramids of solid colour, oranges, apples, grapes moist with liquid drippings, soft peaches itchy to the touch and at the counter a girl, a perfect counterfoil to such depth of colour. Pale white skin on narrow limbs and dark Italian russet head. Her face confirmed this better class of redhead, not Celtic coarse but porcelain pale, translucent yet opaque for no flaw showed. She wore the dark green overall of the old-fashioned greengrocers. At the 'vee' of the neck the outline of her breasts drew his eyes. He felt remembered eroticism, a desire to trace with tongue tip around her body the course of a single violet vein. For the first time his soul moved to his genitals and, caution thrown to the wind, he bought two pounds of granny smiths, one pound of oranges and peaches from the south of France. He returned the next day and the day after for further stock. So began a short-lived obsession.

He pursued his prey cautiously. Not from fear of rejection — his standing as bookshop owner, Jesuit boy and graduate assured acceptance — but class difference, while bolstering confidence, disturbed his vanity. He made his mind up to keep her to himself. He had few friends, and no parents living. He changed her style of dress, buying her simple clothes of dark colour, spending money freely to deck this object of desire. Attempted education revealed doors that could not open so he left her mind alone — not for display. To a man unused to women she seemed a beauty.

He savoured the envious glances of others and his happiness took him by surprise. At times he felt uneasy at such a wide divide between them but her honest admiration and seduction over-rode his doubts. He had his books, his music, the Third programme, the odd acquaintance for mental stimulation. Separation of mind and body was historically respectable.

She was twenty years old and had a highly unsuitable background which he was prepared to overlook. Home was in the seedier section of the South Circular Road, a narrow hall jammed with decaying bikes and chipped linoleum. Mother served his tea and flattered. Father, a minor clerk, pinched with hardwon respectability, doffed his cap. He could do what he liked with them so he rubbed them out.

He married her in Rome. Her parents had to come; he kindly paid their fare; no ghastly Auntie Mary, Uncle Joe or granny from Ringsend, money well spent. Mr. Wolff's sister came from Cheshire. Astonishment stopped short at exchange of glances.

'Do come and stay when you're settled.' Bernadette in the stockbroker belt of Cheshire, never. Acquaintances presumed pregnancy. They were wrong. Carnal knowledge began at midnight on their wedding night and is best passed over. Inexperienced age and nervous youth produce no ecstasy but nature, undeterred by lack of pleasure, takes her toll and nine months later Mr. Wolff's daughter was born.

15

At first he enjoyed fatherhood from a distance. A clean baby with mother in another room so he would not be disturbed. He had established potency and could relax. Of course a boy is more socially rewarding but this little girl was her mother's child pale, and pretty, auburn tendrils around her face, but, wait, one year later look again! Bridget (given in to at a moment of weakness after birth) was a throwback, a reversion to genetic type; red not auburn hair, coarse skin inflamed by teething rash. Arriving in the evenings he was greeted by the flashing buttocks of his monkey child.

'Airing her bottom' Bernadette said. 'The only way to clear up nappy rash.' He left them to the warm breakfast room and requested fires in the drawingroom.

'In the lounge?'

He ground his teeth. After that he liked his meals alone. His life began to centre again on his cultural activities. He renewed his membership of the Royal Dublin Society. The child grew and Bernadette became an Irish mother, albeit of a girl.

So passed the 'sixties. Mr. Wolff ignored the swinging, sex and turbulence of the opening of Pandora's Box. The tidal wave of youth was but an ominous heave on the horizon, but by the 'seventies, there it loomed, the future statistically solid. Bernadette and Bridget were prepared. In the warm kitchen over the years they sucked up the media of initiation. Bernadette secretly worried over Bridget's future in a permissive age, a buyer's market, what price liberation, not even the power of cunt in hand. Mr. Wolff, not into *Cosmopolitan*, cinema, problem pages, the *Late, Late Show*, ignored the revelations. But he could not ignore the physical assault upon his streets.

Living on Seapoint front, a voyeur's paradise on sunny days, for this tropical summer of '76 had yielded a harvest of pulcritude unsurpassed in Irish history. The languid limbs of Ireland's youth entwined on his doorstep. Mr. Wolff's religious susceptibilities were not offended. His ritual Sunday mass was just that, but he suffered from outrage. He gave up walking the beach and sat at week-ends under the garden trees reading the works of another century. His wife, still beautiful, had grown

16

middle-aged with elegance, but his daughter flashed her tits and buttocks in rhythm to the dance of youth. Communication now took the form of scribbled messages on erect nipple.

He did not discuss his observations with Mrs. Wolff. For a number of years now their conversation was limited to essential practicalities. Now that Bridget was nineteen and working in some menial secretarial job, Mrs. Wolff was out a great deal. Her popularity surprised and irritated him, although he recognised she was entitled to time off provided her duties were attended to. He had not sent her from his bedroom, but when a replacement bed was called for, twins seemed appropriate. Union in the narrow physical sense took place at his instigation perhaps once a month and was of no significance. He lived a life of strict routine and like his lunch-time walks in the Green (disturbed by naked flesh) his VAT returns, his *Daily Telegraph,* their monthly coupling was stitched into the overall pattern. He did not know what she did in her free time, apart from visiting her parents. He would not have said she had a life of her own; what life there was was his of which she had a part.

The summer of '76 rolled fiercely to a close. By August Ireland was a parched land. Sun worship had declined and housewives, heavily tanned, withdrew indoors on sunny afternoons and felt no guilt. The mud of Ireland had caked and hardened; soft drink sales soared; butchers complained and picnics were the order of every day. Water was handled with care by the conspicuous, socially responsible. The feckless used it extravagantly and then compensated by 'sharing a bath with a friend'.

Mr. Wolff's life had become uncomfortable. The sun shining in the drawing room window revealed the talcum powder in the air. He had developed a dry nervous cough. He moved into the guest bedroom away from the pressure of his wife's breathing and the embarrassment of her falling skin. She seemed concerned and began to worry about his cough and general health but he refused to see a doctor. In his shop his latest assistant painted her nails and gave him back-answers and, in the midst of works of genius, read *True Romance* and *Woman's Own.* He thought almost fondly of his nose-picking moron who had known her place. She, alas, back in the convent after an unwanted pregnancy contacted at the end of an evening begun in the Crystal would trudge flat foot twixt chapel, parlour and visitors door forever. His books were crumbling around him. He took to leaving jars of water to dispel the dryness and to dip his fingers in from time to time. Samantha looked at him sharply and on Monday when he objected to her jeans handed in her notice.

'I'm going to a record shop — more money and more life.' She whisked her buttocks out.

'No entry.' 'One-way street.' He groaned.

Some nuns arrived to discuss text books. He dreaded the end-of-month queues, the young like locusts swarming, fatter, bigger, every year as they fed upon the bodies of the middle-aged. Even the church had tasted flesh. Nuns in short skirts with upraised eyes, flirtation on their faces. He was not bewildered by the changes. Bewilderment requires an open mind. He was outraged and depressed.

He had begun to fear a transfer of his wife's disease. His skin was painfully dry and had the reptilian look of extreme age. He kept tins of Vaseline around the shop to curb the flaking but not to much avail.

That Monday of Samantha's resignation he left the shop at half-past five. A metal furnace blazed between Dawson Street and home. Seabound girls pressed sweaty bodies against his hot tin box. He could not face home. He became convinced he had not locked the rere of the shop but it hardly mattered. He must escape the crowds. All week he had been dipping himself in water. The pressure in the shop was low but every few minutes he left his dry books to run water over his fingers.

A recurring dream of childhood eased this summer's nights. A picnic in the normal moist July of Ireland by the reservoir in the Wicklow hills, lying in long cool grass, the lap of distant water behind his mother's words, his father swinging sister in the air. He headed for the mountain road.

By now the sun was dipping, adding glare to heat and soon

18

his eyes began to ache. It was quiet at the reservoir. He parked the car and sighing over blistered grass ached for water. When he reached the bank dry rock stretched below, a thin trickle of muddied liquid taunted in the middle. He returned slowly to the car and sat until nightfall drumming his fingers on the wheel and breathing raspily the distress he could not weep.

In the emptied gulf the creaking earth, dry and parched, too long awaited the deluge it would not absorb, and the flood to follow.

Cherubim

Mary Walkin

I WASN'T a bit surprised to see my old pal Lorcan Burke, all biz and importance at the Pope's elbow every turn he made on his visit to Ireland. I knew him immediately even though I haven't seen him in twenty-five years when we both terminated a grand and glorious career as altar boys and went our separate ways in the world. Lorcan went on for the priesthood. He's based in Rome and word has it he'd be the first man to protest modestly that it's completely untrue the Sistine Chapel would fall on the lot of them over there if he withdrew his services tomorrow. He's too young to be a Cardinal or anything like that although he's changed a lot if that is not more the opinion of the cardinal-makers than his own most private. In fact I'd go so far as to say that when the non-Italian Pope was elected, a few decidedly unhumble thoughts flitted between the Burke ears. And how do I know the workings of the hierarchical mind, this hierarchical mind in particular? Didn't I inspect it, explore it, pick it, revere it, emulate it at the only time the Jesuits feel it's worth bothering? And didn't I share the best training there is for a dizzying rise in the church for those so minded? I'm telling you, the hierarchy of altar boys in the town of Duneen was as jealously guarded and subject to protocol as any conclave of princes of the church.

It took years of experience to be a really good altar boy, the talents required being many and varied. You had to make the Latin responses with the finesse of a Cicero, have a light and timely touch on the bells and grace of movement with the cruets and missal stand. Old hands could light or snuff the tallest candle with the slightest touch of the taper and all true professionals had a hidden talent. It was nature that completely belied the angelic countenance that won them the position in the first place, so they could quietly and efficiently fix any fellow who had thoughts of muscling in on their lucrative summer season.

There was no doubt about it. The job was a dead loss all winter. Who wanted to get up and yawn his way through the seven o'clock with Father O'Hehir on a bleak Wednesday in January? Still, it was the price you had to pay to be in the right place in June, when the holiday priests started to arrive for the season. These were quickly put into three categories, the ones who tipped well after each Mass, the ones who tipped a regular server at the end of their stay and those whose method of payment didn't matter a great deal because they believed the vow of poverty extended to altar boys.

So the trick was to spot your priest early on, learn his habits and remember them for next year. Many really good altar boys went on to become superb head waiters when they outgrew their talents in the sacristy.

All through the summer season there would be a continuous stream of Masses on both the side altars as well as the main High Altar. I don't know whether the holidaying priests felt they would lose the knack if they didn't keep their hands in or whether it was part of their rules, but whatever the reason, the traffic on and off the altars all season was heavy.

The green recruits would have a stable of runners whose devotion stretched the Mass into thirty-five minutes or more and whose appreciation was not in keeping. A really top class altar boy wouldn't be seen dead serving such a priest and the king pin would have his own regular priest or two for the season plus about a dozen or so of the better paying casuals. In this the year of Our Lord, nineteen hundred and fifty-five, the king pin was undoubtedly Lorcan Burke and I fancied myself in second position.

'Burke, Lavelle, come here a minute.' Father O'Hehir called to myself and Lorcan one glorious June morning. Father O'Hehir, the parish curate was a firm believer in too many cooks and two women in the kitchen and all that so by 8.30 in the morning, with due charity and courtesy towards the visitors, he was usually out on the first fairway. It was past that now and he was rattling his car-keys and a golf tee with impatience.

'I've a job for the pair of you.' We brightened visibly. Betcha it was to pick the location of the altar boys' outing in September.

'Right, boys. You know you're two of the best I have. Well it's time to put your expertise to good use as it were. Do you know Kevin McEllin?'

'We do,' we said warily. We didn't like the way this was shaping up. 'Well, Kevin wants to become an altar boy, has done for a long time it seems. Brother O'Brien feels it might be a good thing for him and I must say I'm inclined to agree with him.'

We stared in disbelief. Surely Father O'Hehir, of all people, knew that you joined the altar boys when you were seven and worked your way up. Kevin McEllin was thirteen if he was a minute, same age as us. Did he not know that McEllin's mother was the talk of the town for the way she had to be carried home last St. Patrick's Day? For five years it had seemed a good idea to keep him out? Now Father O'Hehir had decided that Kevin McEllin should be an altar boy. What was going on? Father O'Hehir was very busy flicking a mote of earth from his golf tee.

'Brother O'Brien feels it might do Kevin a lot of good to be given a position of trust as it were.' And I'd say it was a good poke in the conscience Father O'Hehir got from Bolshy O'Brien while he was at it, too.

22

'I must say, on thinking about it,' he seemed to be having difficulty clearing his throat, 'I'm inclined to agree with Brother O'Brien. Anyway I know you two will do all you can to smooth the way for Kevin McEllin, I've told him he could call on you for some help with the Latin responses this afternoon. You can expect him at your house about three o'clock, Lorcan, if that's alright with you. He says he's looking forward to it.'

I'll bet he did. That put the tin hat on it. Did Father O'Hehir not know that Kevin McEllin was the leader of the West End Raiders? And for him to enter the home of one of the East End Invaders was the ultimate insult? I think what annoyed and scared us more than anything, however, was the horrible certainty that McEllin had what it took to wrest the position of top earner in the sacristy from Lorcan in about three weeks flat. Where did that leave the summer season?

Kevin McEllin was heard before he was seen that afternoon. We all tied cigarette-box sirens to the spokes of our bicycles, but try as we might, none of us could touch McEllin for racket. He'd even made a paragraph in the *Sligo Champion* for it. One day he was making his noisy way down Main Street, sirens attached, young brother on the crossbar. Sergeant Egan came charging out of the barracks, hitching his braces as he went.

'Get that off your bike, you young pup' he roared. McEllin pushed his terrified young brother off the bar and into the gutter at the sergeant's feet and off on his flapping way with him.

This prestigious event was a sore point with us and McEllin knew it. So when we heard the familiar taunting siren, we fumed in Lorcan's back yard.

'Couldn't we teach him the wrong responses, Lorcan?' I whispered.

'Ah for God's sake, d'ye think he's goin' to sit here like an eejit and let us teach him the wrong responses? What d'ya take him for?'

McEllin propped his bike against neutral property, Doyle's next door, and came whistling up Lorcan's drive.

'We're here, McEllin,' called Lorcan from the back yard. 'Who d'ya think y'are heading for the front doorbell like a visitor?'

McEllin slung his thumbs in the pockets of his jeans and swayed easily from one foot to the other.

'I just came to tell you two bucks, that although it's very kind of you to offer to help me with the Latin, y' can save your breath. I had a half hour to spare this morning, so I ran over them myself.'

Lorcan's chin stuck out. 'You couldn't've learnt them in half an hour, McEllin, you couldn't've.'

'Oh no?' said McEllin softly. 'Try me.'

'Orate fratres, ut meum ac vestrum sacrificium acceptabile fiat apud Deum Patrem omnipotentem.' rattled Lorcan, showing he knew the priest's lines too.

'Suscipiat Dominus sacrificium de manibus tuis ad laudem et gloriam nominus sui, ad utilitatem quoque nostram totiusque Ecclesiae suae sanctae. An' it's great that you know the priest's bit Burke, but it's not an awful lot of good t'ya is it?' McEllin smirked.

'Sursum corda.' hissed Lorcan.

'Habemus ad Dominum' smiled McEllin.

'Gratias agamus Domino Deo nostro.'

'Dignum et justum est.' said McEllin. 'In fact vere dignum et iustum est.'

There was an emphasis on the vere that was downright condescending. Lorcan reddened slowly.

'Alright McEllin, so you know them. But there's one point about becoming an altar boy I'm sure you've forgotten.' Lorcan turned to me. 'Hey Jimmy, do you remember the immortal words of Jesus Christ himself, what was it now? Ah yes, Unless a man be born again of water and the Holy Ghost, he cannot enter the Kingdom of Heaven.'

'God, I do, Lorcan, I do.' said I catching on in delight.

'You can't do anything to me Lorcan Burke. Your mother's in the kitchen. I saw her.'

'You wouldn't want it said now, that you went screamin' to my mother for help, now would you McEllin? would you?

Anyway she thinks we are playing cops and robbers, so she'll be expecting a few yells. But just in case, we'll bring you round to Doyle's for a bit of peace. You know you broke the rules the minute you walked in here, don't you?'

It was two to one, so we dragged him, struggling, through the shrubs into Doyle's garden.

'The Doyles are away on their holliers so ya can yell 'till ya bust, McEllin. Now, as for the Holy Ghost, we can only hope he'll see fit to descend on you, but we can definitely make sure of the water for you.'

We tied him up with Doyle's clothes-line and turned the hose on him. Full.

We knew it was a stop-gap victory, but even then we weren't ready for the speed and efficiency of the counter-attack. When Lorcan arrived to serve Mass on the following Monday, who should be out on the main altar having comman-deered Father Gonzaga but McEllin? Could you credit it? And to add insult to injury he was genuflecting under the weight of the heaviest Missal stand like a Nijinsky. It was an old trick that a new altar boy practised his art with a light wooden Missal stand and his mentors in the senior ranks waited until the day of his first real Mass to substitute the heaviest brass Missal stand they could find. Then yer man would be doing beautifully under the watchful proud gaze of his Mammy in the front rows until it came time to carry the Missal down the altar steps, genuflect and up the right side for the Gospel. For this, with proper soulful humility, he'd exert exactly the amount of pressure he'd learned was necessary to lift his burden, only that pressure was now right to toss the Missal over his shoulder and with any luck knock himself off-balance into the bargain. Great stuff for keeping the new hands in the size of boots that befitted them but McEllin had obviously heard all about it. Not only was he sailing through with the heaviest stand, but he was serving the greatest prize in the sacristy, Father Gonzaga.

Father Gonzaga kept the same altar boy for the month and slipped him a whole pound the day he left. Not only was he the most generous, but he was never a second over twenty minutes on the altar and he always told you what time he'd need you the next day. Even the congregation knew him for a good thing. If anyone was attending a Mass that wasn't too far through when Gonzaga started, they'd be over to his altar like a shot.

Lorcan watched in fury from the sacristy. He'd had Father Gonzaga last year and the year before. I wished I could have cheered him up by pointing out failings of McEllin's but his performance was well above par. He knelt at exactly the right spot and his bells were timely and just loud enough. He was at Father Gonzaga's elbow with the cruets a second before he needed them and his responses were devout and clear. Lorcan was so upset when he heard Father Gonzaga making arrangements with McEllin for the following morning, that he let a fairly decent Canon slip through his fingers to Shorty Thompson.

Now I'm a loyal fellow to my friends and proud of it, but I have to admit, Lorcan Burke pushed me to the limits the next few days. Not only was McEllin in the first place, but Lorcan wasn't even looking like competition. It killed me to see McEllin's smirk spreading as even the greenest little twerps were beginning to poach on Lorcan's territory.

'Janey Mac, Lorcan' I protested mildly, 'Would you ever do something, anything. Maybe McEllin is the best, but you don't have to retire altogether.'

'Shut up, Lavelle, I'm thinkin'. And don't let me hear you sayin' a stupid thing like that again, d'ya hear me? Unless ya want to be pickin' yer teeth outa your tonsils.'

I let that pass on account of the many years of friendship between us and because I didn't want to kick a fellow when he was down. So I kept to myself then and concentrated on my own clientele, so to speak. I didn't know what to expect when Lorcan said to pass the word around the senior altar boys to stay back after all the priests had gone the next Monday.

There must have been about twelve of us in the sacristy, including McEllin. Lorcan held up his hand for silence.

'I think it's obvious to everyone here that Kevin McEllin and I can't both be altar boys.' I was very proud of him then.

He sounded just like Gary Cooper in *High Noon*. At the same time, I was terrified Lorcan was hoping he'd be as lucky as Gary Cooper.

'I agree with that, Lorcan Burke' said McEllin, 'and I'm glad to see you know when you're licked.'

'Well maybe I am, McEllin an' then maybe I'm not. What I'd like is a fair fight for it.'

'Oh yeh? And then Father O'Hehir gets to hear of it and we're both drummed out of it? Not likely, Burke. Nothing doing.'

'I never meant a common brawl, McEllin, although I daresay that is all you'd understand. No, what I had in mind was a fair peaceful contest and the loser retires.'

'What kind of contest?' said McEllin suspiciously.

'I'll race you on the altar. Any priest of yours against any priest of mine.'

'You mean I can choose any priest at all?'

'Sure thing. We each choose our man and then agree on three fellows to time us.'

'You're on, Lorcan Burke. You're on. And my choice is Father Gonzaga,' said McEllin triumphantly.

'Fine,' said Lorcan as I looked helplessly on. Lorcan had lost before he'd started. No one, but no one was faster than Father Gonzaga. For a wild minute I thought he might have bribed his cousin, Father Patrick, to come down from Dublin and gallop through a Mass for him, but his next words floored me altogether.

'Grand choice, McEllin and mine is Canon Fennessy.'

Hisses, cheers and groans went up depending on whose side their owner was. As for me, I thought Lorcan had finally and completely lost his mind. Canon Fennessy was eighty-seven years old, there being no retiring age for priests at this time. He insisted on saying Mass every single morning and was never known to be off the altar in less than forty-five minutes. It took him nearly five minutes alone to totter from the sacristy to the side altar, his fuzzy steel hair like malignant earmuffs under his canon's hat. His head got there considerably in advance of the rest of him and he had a drool a St. Bernard would envy. He sometimes refused Communion on such paltry grounds as the communicant's having too small a mouth or one sporting lipstick. On other occasions he attempted to administer it to pillars. Needless to say, when Canon Fennessy was ready to say Mass, only the very rawest of servers were to be seen.

Lorcan was calmly dictating the terms of the agreement.

'Tomorrow morning, July, the third, 1955, a contest will be held to see who gets off the altar fastest, Father Gonzaga served by Kevin McEllin, or Canon Fennessy served by Lorcan Burke. The server of the slower celebrant then agrees to retire from altar service.'

Lorcan and McEllin duly signed the agreement and McEllin began hinting that a few bets might be in order. Nobody was willing to make bets although McEllin was offering five to one on Lorcan and Canon Fennessy. The floor was almost closed when Lorcan took a half-crown out of his pocket and took McEllin up on his offer. We took this as the last proof of his madness.

The next morning, Father Gonzaga was first off the mark. Three of us stood in the sacristy door, our watches synchronised. In exactly eighteen minutes and fourteen seconds, Father Gonzaga and a smug McEllin genuflected as they passed the main alter on the home straight.

The priests must have been a bit puzzled that morning. The sacristy was like Aintree before the Grand National, yet when they were ready to say Mass, there wouldn't be a server in sight except the youngest ones who were as wise as themselves. There wasn't room to move when at last Canon Fennessy took up his chalice for the lurch to the far side altar. I took the time despairingly and the last thing Lorcan whispered to me was that if McEllin should offer double or quits, he'd break my face if I didn't accept on his behalf.

Seven minutes and we were still on the Confiteor. Canon Fennessy always had about three stabs at it before he got through it. Twelve minutes and we were struggling with the Collect. I needn't tell you he didn't make up time on the Epistle and Gospel.

'I don't suppose you want to make that double or quits do ya Lavelle?' McEllin was sneering at my elbow.

My half-crown was lovely and big and warm in my pocket. But what does it profit a man if he doesn't lay down his half-crown for his friend?

'Begod I do, McEllin. You haven't won yet y'know. Double or quits it is. You haven't won yet.'

'You're off your head, Lavelle. They've four and a half minutes to go and they haven't even started the offertory.'

I knew McEllin was right. I turned back to watching, sick at the thought of McEllin taking our money, pride and Lorcan's only means of support. Thank God at least Canon Fennessy wasn't going for the Credo. He shuffled around to face the congregation and chanced spreading out his arms. The effort was too much for his concentration. He looked at Lorcan.

'Dominus vobiscum' hissed Lorcan.

'Dominus vobiscum' wavered Canon Fennessy.

'Et cum spiritu tuo' came the devout response from Lorcan.

Canon Fennessy made to turn back. A gentle whisper came from Lorcan. Canon Fennessy swayed, his ear bent. His eyebrows rose and he made a little O with his mouth, his face clouded with indecision. Up wobbled his arms in blessing.

'Ite Missa est' he pronounced emphatically.

'Deo Gratias' rang out Lorcan, while McEllin danced around me like a man watching his horse fall at the last fence.

'Ite missa est? Go the Mass is ended? He's after making him skip three quarters of it. That's not fair . . . .' I was jumping up and down restraining a mad urge I had to do a circuit of the high altar shouting. 'Go home, go home. Didn't ye hear the Canon . . . Go home the Mass is ended . . .'

I didn't have to. Lorcan's timing was perfect. Canon Fennessy hadn't yet uncovered the chalice for the offertory. He picked it up and began the stretch for the sacristy, preceded by Lorcan. Lorcan, a saintly expression on his face, his years of experience about his head like a halo.

The Day
It All Ended

Carla Goldberg

IT WAS a soft April morning. The sun shone on the wet grass and the early morning rain was still glistening on the hedges. The lawns in the gardens he passed looked like silver velvet. The boy admired them, thinking how they looked soft and warm, not damp and chilly as he knew them to be. They looked like the bag his *zeide* used for his *tefillin,* as old and gently grey as the old man himself. He quickened his pace. The others would be in shul long since. It was Shabbas, a lovely soft Shabbas, and he was not far past thirteen. He had lingered over breakfast, talking to his mother, making faces at the baby, letting the others leave without him. Now, he would be late. The old men would look sideways at him and at each other and nod their heads. He skipped to a run, whistled, remembered himself and stopped, whistled again. The morning was fine, it was Saturday and he was thirteen.

On the corner by the shul, he passed a news stand. He stopped a moment to read the headline. *He* was in town, making speeches and promises; the streets were full of him. A big photograph of him was on the front of the day's paper. There he stood, in his greatcoat, with his strong face almost smiling. The boy considered it. It was bigger than the picture he had on his bedroom wall, but then, that was in colour and this was only newsprint. Still . . . he put his hand in his pocket, but it was Shabbas, so he had no money. He grinned to himself. Imagine coming into shul with the paper under his arm! His uncle would create such a fuss, and then all the others would notice, and pretend not to see like the time the visitor from the States came in without a *yarmulka*.

He walked on, composing himself to look suitably serious and humble and quiet, and less like a boy in from a run on a sunny spring morning. He fished his *yarmulka* out of his pocket and stuck it on his head. He slipped in quietly and sat beside his other uncle, Uncle Simon who wasn't so strict, who owned a big, black limousine and was suspected of occasionally conducting business on Shabbas. He sat very quiet to still his breathing before he even tried to find his place in the service.

The big man leaned back in the shiny limousine and relaxed. He paid no attention to the passing countryside. In his hand he held a sheaf of papers. He had his speech, carefully typed by the clerk, and a list of the current problems and talking points in the area, together with some thoughts his aide had scribbled in on each one.

'Just some suggestions, Sir,' the aide had said, his liquid brown eyes adoring. The man was running through them in his head. He never spoke from a script. He was commonly believed to speak completely ad lib and this added to his reputation. In fact, he never spoke off the cuff, or let himself get into the position of having to give an impromptu opinion. He was always prepared for any question that might arise. Of course, here it was easy: this was his own country, he knew every stick and stone, every trick the weather could play, every mood of the fishing season. His aides had briefed him about the harvest, the poachers, the luck of the herring fleets, but even without that, he would have been safe. Hadn't his cousin written to welcome him, saying how they all relied on him to do something about land tenure and rents and rates and the state of the hospital and the rainfall last summer? He flicked through his notes again briefly, then handed them to the aide sitting beside him, not the one with the melting chocolate eyes but a local man, dour and somewhat shifty.

The man leaned back more comfortably and looked out the window. He noticed the prosperity of the farms they passed, the size of the herds grazing the lush meadows, the amount of ploughing done. A cluster of children standing on a gate shouted and waved. The driver slowed down, maybe for the children, maybe for the sharpness of the bend. The wheels spun briefly, catching the mud at the verge. The man smiled on the children, raised his hand almost in blessing, unconsciously imitating the prelates he had seen ride by all his life.

'Even the young children want to see you, Sir,' said the aide. His voice revealed the respect that his face hid. The man nodded and smiled.

'They don't understand,' he said. 'They believe what their parents tell them.'

'And their teachers. The teachers are doing great work. Of course, they have to tread warily. There's still some about here . . .' His silence told of blood as yet unshed, battles still unfought.

The man grunted. It was good to get out to the remote areas again. Back in the city, the political maelstrom caught a man up and he lost the clear, uncompromising vision of the idealist. Even last night, in the town, he had felt the vigour, the unwillingness to settle for less. Now, on his way to his power base, the place where he was born, where his first victories and defeats had been. He felt he was returning to a well of pure strength. He lit a cigarette.

It was a long drive. The road deteriorated as they went further into the heartland. The houses became poorer, the churches smaller, the land rougher. Suddenly, rounding a corner and cresting a hill, he saw the sea ahead and knew they had arrived. He felt a thrill of anticipation, now, when he was to meet his own people, the people with whom he had grown up, who had sent him out as their representative, their champion for the new order.

32

The big black limousine coasted down the hill into the village, past the graveyard where the man's mother had lain this twenty years. There were people in the street, some going about their daily business, others clearly there for the occasion. They were standing looking up the hill. When the car came over the top, they had started waving. Now they were shouting, the shoppers were turning, women were coming out of the houses, drawing their shawls around them as they came onto the street. Children, everywhere children, pouring out of alleyways, leaping, shouting, waving. It was seven years since he had been home. His heart beat faster.

The car slowed to a walking pace. He rolled down the window, compelled by the eager faces beyond the glass. They called, shouted, thrust hands in at him. The aide in the front seat tensed.

'Welcome home,' the voices cried, glad voices. Who said a prophet was without honour in his own country? For the moment, he revelled in this emotional out-pouring, this sharing in the glory of the man who had come from them, had gone to battle for them and had triumphed. He knew the hard talk would come later, the demands, the orders. The tone would change. There would be less joy in the past, more bargains, more promises for the future.

'We put you there,' they would say. 'Now, this is what you have to do.' But that was not yet. Now, he could just smile and wave and say 'God bless you' and after lunch would be time to get tough.

The car stopped outside the only hotel in the village. It was really only a public house that could serve food. Still, it was the best the village had, and if he had grown used to better, he was able to conceal the thought.

The driver drew the car up in such a way that there was only a pace from the door into the hotel. The two aides came and stood one on either side as the big man got out of the car, beaming, acknowledging the crowd. He patted a child's head. All the time his eyes were searching. He saw no face other than friendly, smiling women, excited youngsters. The men would stay away till later. He vanished into the house, leaving the crowd expectant, still unfulfilled. The door slammed. Inside, he met the local organisation men. No one else had been allowed in. Not even some of his childhood friends whom he dearly wanted to meet, and who had entreated an audience. The organisation had been adamant. Childhood friends can be manhood enemies and many a hero had been done to bloody death by a blood brother.

There was food and drink and serious matters to be dealt with before the meeting, the speeches, the rally in the afternoon. As they ate and drank and argued, the sounds of ass carts and horses and tramping feet could be heard in the street. The village was filling up. The people were coming in from the outlying hamlets and scattered townlands to hear the great man speak, to voice their complaints, to see with their own eyes the living legend of their times.

The boy walked home for lunch between his father and his brother. They told him he had been late, he must have been dawdling, idling, thinking of things other than the Sabbath. They remarked how the chazan was not on form today, perhaps his chest was troubling him again, cain an hara. They said hallo, good Shabbas to Hymie the furrier, whom they hated. They came to the news-stand.

'That man's in town,' said his father. 'That's what all the police were in town for. I was wondering.'

'He's not in town now,' said the boy. 'He's gone down to speak in his own place.'

'Down there? Brave man.'

Uncle Simon caught them up. He was to come to lunch, his wife and children being out of town.

'Did you see that man's in town?' asked the father.

'No. He's out in the country. He's gone to visit his own folks. I should know. He went in my best limousine. The party men came and hired it yesterday. For tomorrow, too. Cash in advance. Nice job.'

The father scowled at this almost-mention of business, but he was impressed, too. 'He's a great man and no doubt,' he allowed.

'Ah yes, it's a *mitzvah*. A real *mitzvah* to rent the car to

34

him. I'm proud he's in it.'

'I thought he always went in an armoured car,' said the brother.

'That's what I said myself, I said it to them when they came in to me. "I thought he used an armoured car," I said. Now, most of all, after what happened to his deputy.'

'What did they say?' asked the boy eagerly.

'Well, they said he does, especially now. So he came down last night in his armoured car, but he wasn't going visiting his own people in one. It would look bad, like maybe he didn't trust them.'

'Hmph,' snorted the father. 'I would think that's where he'd need protection most. When you've family, who needs enemies?'

The men laughed. The boy didn't understand.

'Why d'you say that?' he asked. 'Surely his own people should be most proud of him?'

'It's not that, boy,' said the uncle. 'It's just a fact of life.' The boy still didn't understand. He was only thirteen. He let it go.

'He's a great man, all the same,' said the father.

'Yes. Give him a few years, and we'll all have a bit of peace.'

'No more fighting. It's bad for business.'

The uncle nodded. They were nearly home. 'Ah, yes. Quiet times. That's what we all need. Them and us. When times are good, they don't notice us. They discover their charity.' He drawled the last word. The father shrugged. The two sons listened, scuffing the stones with their feet.

'Yes,' agreed the father. 'That's what we all need. Peace. Ohse shalom . . . This town, this country, it's been torn apart. We're all tired of the killing. We all need peace.' He pushed the gate and turned up his front path. He sniffed the air. 'It's a fine day for a run in the country.'

Inside, the house was warm and smelt of cholent and chicken soup. The smaller children ran to meet them from the kitchen, dressed in their best, excited at a visit from their uncle. He had presents for them all, tucked away in his jacket.

The father pretended not to notice. They were only small gifts, coloured pencils, rubbers, tops, tokens for the children. His sister, the boy's mother, came out and kissed him.

'Good Shabbas. What news from Rachel?'

'She's fine. Arrived safely. All the family's well.'

They sat round the table with the bright white linen cloth. The father blessed the meal and they ate and ate and ate. There was chicken soup with pirogen and chopped liver and cholent and loxchen pudding and tea and pomerantzen. The meal took hours. The children were silent but the two men talked and talked. They discussed politics and the weather and zionism and America and whether to stay where they were.

'Ach,' said Simon. Where's to go?'

Then they discussed where they would like to be, where the climate was right and it was easy to be a Jew and whether there was any future here or there.

The boy left the table. The men were just talking, drinking tea through sugar lumps, waiting for evening and havdalah and then they would talk business before the end of the day.

The boy sat in the curve of the big bay window and admired his stamp collection. For his last birthday, when he had been thirteen, he had been given this new stamp album. He had also received mountains of cards from relatives in foreign parts, America, Germany, Poland, places on maps. Now he had finished soaking them, separating them carefully from the cheap envelopes, trying not to splash the faces of the stamps, not to fade the bright colours or smudge the precious postmarks. The evening sun came slanting through the trees at the end of the garden gilding the table, the candle-stick, the boy's hair.

It was late afternoon when the man got back into the car. There would be another meeting in town and he could not afford to be late. He would gladly have stayed all evening here in his own place, where the people were more interested in the price of cattle and the fishing limits than in the more complex, less soluble issues that were, in fact, his business.

The meeting had gone well. There had been more approval than he had expected. The atmosphere had been of a fair day, with the jostling and shoving and the crying of the donkeys and the smell of horses. It had been good to come, to re-assert the connection with his power base.

Now, as the black limousine breasted the hill, he relaxed. He had no speeches to make tonight, no audience to win. Tonight would be discussion and he would be the listener. Like Solomon judging his people, he thought.

The green of the grass was darker, the shadows deep pools of mystery. A flock of crows overhead flew cackling to their colony, dark prophets in the gathering gloom.

They approached the sharp bend where the children had waved to him that morning. The driver slowed down, whether remembering the earlier welcome or feeling some other presentiment. The corner was sharp, the road muddy from homeward cows. As they rounded the bend at walking speed, a quick burst of gun-fire surprised them all. The windows of the limousine exploded in running stars. The driver braked sharply.

'Drive on, you fool, drive on!' cried the foremost aide, fumbling for his gun in his jacket. The car stalled and refused to start. The driver broke into a stream of abuse as he mangled the self-starter.

The two aides were out in the road, sheltered by the car doors, shooting towards the trees. The crows flew up into the air screeching. The man also carried a gun. It was loaded and ready. He had not been separated from it for many years. He listened to the sound of shooting. He opened his door and slipped out, crouching behind it for cover. The engine caught and purred into life.

'We'll fight the bastards,' said the man. 'There's no more than two of them.'

'Get back in the car,' growled the dour faced aide. 'We'll be round the corner before the bastards can break cover.'

The three were firing methodically. The driver cowered behind the wheel of the car muttering.

'Get back in the car, you crazy bastards, get back in the car, you crazy bastards.'

There was a whine and a thwack as a bullet struck the car, ricocheted, ploughed deep through the man's skull, lodged in his medulla. He crumpled. Cursing, the aide flung himself across the inside of the car, dragged his leader in.

'Get us out of here,' he yelled. The other threw himself in. The car leapt away, doors banging. A rattle of gun-fire followed them but they soon out-distanced it.

The aide in the front seat looked back.

'Oh, Christ,' he said.

The news reached the town with the body, but it flew through the streets like a flash fire. Men left their gardens, women their kitchens. Small children stopped their games.

The boy was in shul. They were nearing the end of *ma'ariv*. They heard the running in the streets, the shouting. Some of the older men had heard such sounds before. They looked at each other, grey old men in a grey light. The boy heard the cry. His sharper ears and better command of the language made out the words — dead — death — murder. He stood up, stretched taut as a strung bow-string. He looked round with wild eyes. One by one, they understood, muttered, whispered, glance met glance in despair. They all stood for *kaddish*.

After the service, they gathered in knots half in, half out of the building. The boy's brother was sent for a paper. No one asked how he happened to have money in his pocket. The evening paper told very little, only the barest facts in the stop-press corner. They murmured and muttered, afraid to ask what this might mean for them.

The boy slipped away as the congregation broke up. He slipped away from his father, his brother, his uncles. He turned towards the centre of the town. He ran through the streets, one long-limbed boy among many. It seemed all the people in the town were going the same way, to the place where the man was laid out, waiting for a hearse to bring him to the city.

38

No one had known what to do with the body. The driver had brought them back to the hotel where the meeting should have been. He had been paid to end the journey there. Neither of the aides had given him any other instructions. They had sat silent in the car until they reached the outskirts of the town. Then, they had briefly discussed the best plan. None seemed worth the effort.

The boy arrived with the crowd in the wide forecourt. There, in the middle, the tides of people swelling past it, stood his uncle Simon's shiny black limousine, its windows shattered, its paintwork chipped. He drew near, carried by the crowd, drawn by the horror. He came close, looked in the window. There was very little blood.

The crowd flowed back and forwards. No one said much. Some of the men were crying. It had been decided to take the man's body to the capital that night, straight away, to remove the focus of revolt. Who knew what could happen? The lying in state would take place in the national cathedral, and then there would be a state funeral. Down here, feelings ran higher, would be less easy to control. The fanatics would follow the body and, being isolated, would be easier to eliminate.

A soft rain fell. The boy stood near the door watching, like everyone else, waiting for something to happen. No one had come out to tell the people anything. There was a loud honking and a polished black hearse pushed its way through the crowd to the main door. Two tall men in black pulled out a coffin as though it were a pile of worsted and carried it into the building. The crowd gasped in unison. They were beginning to understand.

Someone started singing a hymn. Slowly, the refrain was caught, carried by the rest. The boy stood, the one silent spot in the dark echoing courtyard.

Ages passed, and nothing happened. Then, suddenly, without warning, the doors opened. A man came out, a shifty man with a dour look. He spoke briefly about the tragedy that had occurred. His eyes were wide and hollow. They read more in his face than he spoke in his words. He told them the hearse would carry the man's corpse to the station where a train was waiting to take it to the capital. There would be a big funeral, a national day of mourning. The crowd growled with resentment. Even in death, their hero was to be taken away from them. They looked at one another and shifted their feet but there was no leader. The only man who had ever crystallised their action was now being lowered into his hastily commandeered oak coffin.

The speaker went back in. There was a dull silence for a while, then people started talking low. How had it happened? Who had done it? What would be done now? The boy heard angry words and was afraid.

The great doors opened wide and several sombre-faced men appeared, followed by four men carrying the coffin. There was no solemnity, no sense of occasion. They hurried down the steps and threw it into the back of the hearse. The boy put out his hand and touched the shiny wood as it passed close by his face. He was of the House of Aaron, but he never thought of that. He only thought how hollow the box sounded, how it bounced slightly when it struck the platform in the hearse. He never noticed the absence of flowers for his people never put flowers on a coffin.

The driver got into his seat, and an evidently armed man sat in beside him. The other aides, all with guns in their hands, climbed onto the running boards on either side and hung in there.

'What bloody good is that now?' mocked the man next to the boy. The boy looked up into his face and saw tears.

Slowly, the hearse moved away. At walking pace, it pushed gently through the crowd which parted before it, filled in behind. As it came into the street, it was heading a slow procession that grew and grew.

The boy was almost touching the hearse. In the watery street-light, he could see the gleam on the wooden coffin, and the empty brass nameplate. Around him, men were muttering prayers that he did not know. They all held their hats in their hands, turning them round and round in twitching fingers. The boy put his hand in his pocket to pull out his yarmulka, had it half way to his head, remembered where he was, put it back.

They reached the station. The hearse drove right onto the platform. The police tried to keep the people back but they pressed on, a great flood of grief. They came between the hearse and the train, hands reaching out to the coffin as it was man-handled to the goods compartment. The armed men got in and the engine whistled.

'Stand clear! Stand clear! The train is moving.'

Passengers looked out of carriage windows to see what the delay was, why the evening train to the capital was held up so long. The rumour ran like a sigh.

The signals clanged. The whistle blew. The boy stood at the edge of the platform watching the lights dwindling in the distance. The crowd began to break up. There was no trouble yet. The people just melted away into the damp night. The boy was the last, standing on the empty platform staring into the blackness.

'C'mon now, home with you.' The station-master was closing up for the night. The boy ran through the dark and silent streets, crying as he ran.

'*Yisgadal v'yis kadash* – oh what is going to happen to us *allshmay raba* – oh what is going to happen to *us* all?'

The Day
of the
Christening

Harriet O'Carroll

MRS. MORRISEY got up at six o'clock on the morning of the christening. It was her usual time to get up, she did not feel it a hardship. She could get things to rights better when she had the place to herself. She moved quietly in the kitchen of the sleeping house, taking the marmalade pot, sugar bowl and milk jug from the cupboard to the table. He couldn't complain about his breakfast, at any rate. Since the day after they got married it had been on the table for him at a quarter to eight, day in day out, save only the times she was in having the children. He couldn't complain, but he would. Reason and right had never stopped him doing anything he wanted to do. His allegiance was to the football field and the gathered cronies in the scruffy shadows of the pub. If he had a skinful the night before he would call the sausages raw or burnt, whatever they looked like. Or he would get up at twelve and mutter morosely while he waited for them to be warmed up for him. She didn't listen to what she didn't want to hear. If you weren't going to make a hole in the rock, why bruise your head by banging. She had bruised herself enough in the early days. There was no sense in dwelling on what was past, and beyond cure. For years now she had been too busy to rake over rights and wrongs, and just as well too, because surely she had no judgement.

She had thought her last outrage would have cried to the Lord God Himself, for vengeance. She thought even distant connections would have been enraged to the point of violence. She would not have been surprised at balls of fire and thunderbolts. She thought there might have been boycott, bloodletting and imprisonment. But it turned out instead to be a small matter. There was a court appearance, one headline in a local paper, and a few blows after the pubs had closed. She had seen more trouble over a doped greyhound.

The baby was still asleep, that was one mercy. He was a quiet little fellow so far; he made it through the night. She remembered how she had walked the floor with his mother. It did not seem a week ago. A small squalling nervous thing, she had been, tiny arms akimbo at every rustle, noisy dismay at every disturbance. Mrs. Morrisey thought sometimes she must have walked in her sleep, up and down the narrow space, whispering softly and frantically,

'Hush now give over, off to sleep, baby baby, sleepybys, off to sleep, off to sleep, off to sleep.'

She could still feel the fatigue in her bones, head nodding, knees bending, craving and drying and sighing for sleep, whisper fading and trailing, the feeling of a fine wax on her face and the terror in case the three year old would wake too, and the whole night would be gone, neither one settling until daytime was there to be faced again. She had moved then as if to stop would be to die, and she hadn't lost the habit since. She did casual hours at the hotel, serving at winter functions, or cleaning after summer visitors, and she was known as a good worker, an honest woman and an awful talker. Talking was better than thinking any day, and there wasn't a house on the road that did not have its trouble.

'God between us and all harm.'

If Morrisey wasn't the best, maybe he wasn't the worst either. If he did not give her a penny, at least he did not knock her about, she could close her ears to his talk, and what was it to her what he did outside the house. She took care not to find out.

She wondered would Rosaleen ever marry now. Who would have her? And why should she? She had the baby. If she could finish her schooling and get some sort of job, wouldn't she be better off the way she was. It was little of her father's money had put the clothes on her back, or the food on her plate. It was all done by her own scrubbing and cleaning and later on the hours at the factory, not enough time in any day. Mrs. Morrisey took the airing racks away from in front of the dead ashes and folded the clothes in tidy single heaps. She had a few things soaking and she would have time to rinse them out and get them on the line before she slipped out to Mass. Sunday, Monday, she had things on the line, chasing all the time to catch up or to get a little work in hand. The mist was on the sloping fields when she went out. It would be a fine Autumn day, a fine day for it anyway, as people said about a wedding or a funeral. It would be a fine day for the christening of her first grandchild.

She took a look in at Rosaleen and the baby before she left. They were both asleep, mother and child, two children. She turned her eyes quickly away from Rosaleen's pallor and the old lines that should have no place on a fourteen year old face. She focussed instead on the baby. He was sleeping as though he would never wake, impregnable in his unconsciousness, with that soft serene aura that even the ugliest sleeping baby wears. He was not an ugly little fellow. Thank the Lord God in Heaven, he was all right, at least as far as one could see. No twisted foot, no cleft palate, no deformity had been visited on them. That final horror at least they were spared.

It was three quarters of a mile into town. She often said that if she put her shoes at the gate, they would walk there themselves, so used would they be to the journey. She didn't feel it going in to Mass on a fine morning, but the weary journeys home, laden with the things from the shop, or bone tired after scrubbing someone's floor, or worst of all frantic with worry in case the child left behind was smothering in the cot, these trips were twice as long. The road all seemed uphill, all the steps were an effort. Time and again she had put together enough for a bicycle, and every time there was another call on the money. Now the girls were big enough to carry the messages home for her. Her legs had held out when she needed them.

They usually got away with a short sermon at early Mass. Next month would be November, the month of the dead. She would be ritually reminded of her father, slipping away into childhood and coma and death, and of Morrisey's mother, struggling and straining and hanging on. She took five years to go, moaning, haranguing and tormenting in every clear minute. Mrs. Morrisey found it hard to be edified by the prospect of death. She hadn't time to die. Morrisey too, she thought, was made of some material that would hang on until the bitter end. Like a rock, or a malignant weed, he would last her out. The great trouble with Mass was that it gave her time to think. She said over her beads with determination. A long time ago she used to say in Confession, 'I let my thoughts stray in my prayers'. Her thoughts had strayed then to pleasure and prospect, eyeing handsome shoulders in the pews ahead. Her thoughts were now threatened with floodtides of resentment. When she saw the school mistress at the door, she knew it was a sign of no ordinary trouble. For ordinary trouble the schoolmistress would have sent for her.

'No point in going over that now', she said to herself. 'What's done is done.'

'Lamb of God, who takest away the sins of the world, grant us peace' It was nearly over, not much more to go.

'Count your blessings' Mrs. Morrisey told herself.

Morrisey at least had given her the four girls, beautiful girls too, each in her own way. She supposed that her two boys were also blessings. She had fretted over them as much as she ever had over the girls. They were their father's sons and hard as nails. The girls though, had carried the load with her, they had seen what needed to be done. A world that contained Maura, Rita, Rosaleen and Nora could never be completely black.

In three hours she would be back here for the christening.

The baby would be called Michael and where would he belong? There were those in the village who thought she should have said nothing, and sent Rosaleen away. She knew there were some who said it behind her back, and there were others who said it again and again to her face.

'Yerra Maggie, least said soonest mended. You can't undo what's done, what do you want to spread it abroad for? Think of the child.'

'Rosaleen is my child first.'

'Listen here Maggie, what about her schoolmates. You don't expect her to face them, do you?'

'Better to face them out than to know they're whispering. It's no use talking, Rosaleen is not going away.'

And they finally stopped talking to her face, though she knew that still the gossip flourished and elaborated. An already cruel and incredible story became even more fantastic and unbelievable, embellished with the personal style of every teller. It was a cause of shock, a cause of scandal, a cause of evil glee, a cause of ribald speculation, supposedly also a cause of compassion and sympathy.

Morrisey said nothing. She had prepared to tell him with feelings of foreboding and dread, but as the words came out she felt an odd vindictive glee. The piece of bacon was half-way to his lips when she said.

'Your fine bucko, Connors has raped our Rosaleen. She is expecting his kid.'

He put down the fork and walked straight out. She sat at the table, head in hands. She looked at the skin on the grease congealing on the plate. To think she had once thought that when she had him away from his miserable taunting old mother, he would soften and grow. What a thick deluded idiot she had been, and still was to have linked her life like that. He wouldn't say a word to her, no more than if she had never spoken. She could as well have climbed the nearest hill and howled the words to the night wind. He would eat and work and drink and fuck and sleep as he had always done and not a thousand years would shake him alive. She heard afterwards of the brawl outside the pub, but not of anything said. The next

46

time she saw Connors he did not show any obvious signs of ill treatment. She turned away her head as if confronted with a nauseating wound.

'Go, you are dismissed, go in peace.'

Mass was over, and she would be in time to get back and have breakfast on the table. Rosaleen was filling bottles in the kitchen when she came in.

'He's not stirring yet, Mam. He had a bottle at five o'clock. Four ounces, he took. He should be alright until half nine, and if I give him another at half eleven, he should be alright for the christening.'

Rosaleen was already on the old protective treadmill, no way of looking back. She was tied to this small independent life, loving and hating her bondage by turns. She was separated from her age group by maternity as she never could be by sexual knowledge.

The house felt warm and small after the open road. The steam from the kettle was suffocating Mrs. Morrisey. She threw open the small kitchen window.

'I was ever a one for air' she said. 'Don't you feel it close, Rosy?'

'I didn't notice it' said Rosaleen. 'Will you have some tea if I wet it? No one is moving yet.'

Mrs. Morrisey sat and drank tea with her daughter, and told her who was at Mass and what they were wearing and who was prayed for, having died during the week.

'Who would have expected Jimmy Mullen to go like that. He could only be fifty-eight, and him a fine fresh coloured man, wasn't he in past the house to the creamery not much more than a week ago. And not chick nor child to take over that fine place. It will probably go to a nephew if it isn't sold up altogether.'

And all the time she talked she wondered how it was that she had never noticed that Rosaleen was pregnant, and had to be told by the schoolteacher. She hadn't found it in her to believe it, and yet was too stunned to deny. That day too, the room had become suddenly hot, the delph and the dresser and the mantlepiece had swam round her, and as they settled, she

47

heard the voice saying

'I'm afraid you'll have to prepare yourself for a shock. The father is a married man.'

'Tell me then, in the name of God.'

She couldn't think who it could be, Morrisey's gormless boozing crony was the last to occur to her. The schoolmistress was a strong woman with a fine family. They had stuck to their books, grown up, and taken their degrees. They were married now, or in the Civil Service, settled respectably. She had been in control of the situation all her life. She looked at Mrs. Morrisey with useless sympathy. She felt as if in the presence of terminal illness, words of alleviation were of no avail, the only grim solace lay in outfacing the stony fact. Life would go on, until it ceased.

'I don't think any of her classmates know. She did not really know herself, at least, she was hoping it couldn't be so. She has only the vaguest idea of . . . you know. If it wasn't for the pregnancy I don't suppose anyone would ever have known what went on. She was afraid to say, you see.'

'I never saw a thing, myself.'

'She started going pale in class. Then I found her being sick one day. After that I kept my eyes open and I finally persuaded her to speak to me.'

Mrs. Morrisey still wondered what Rosaleen had said to the teacher. The subject was too thick with rocks, she kept away. To Rosaleen she had said,

'Why did you not tell me?'

'I don't know. What could I say?'

'Do you want to stay at home, or do you want to go away?'

'Oh Mam, I want to stay home.'

'That's that so.'

So Rosaleen stayed home, and when the child was born, there was no word of bringing him anywhere but home. Morrisey could do what he chose, and he chose to do nothing.

Rosaleen's three sisters and two brothers came to the christening, and Morrisey too stayed on after late Mass. The church was all empty and echoing as the words were said that made the child a Christian. It was done so quickly and it was done for life.

Morrisey wanted his lunch for half past one, at the latest. There was a football match he couldn't miss, but the meat and soup were on the range since before they all went to the Church. The potatoes were peeled, and the cabbage would boil in no time. If he was late itself, thought Mrs. Morrisey, he had not much to complain of, one day in how many years? Rita had the table set, and mercifully the baby settled down again after his experience. Maybe he wouldn't stir until they were all fed. Finally the eight of them were sitting down, and she herself last of all; when the truly unusual and cataclysmic event occurred.

Mrs. Morrisey looked at the two slices of beef and the dark green cabbage, and the brown gravy against the potatoes. Unexpectedly, without precedent, without rhyme or reason she began to cry. The tears fell first, almost before she, or anyone else knew it, then gathering force, great warm heavings spread down through her neck, throat and chest. Her skin throbbed, her face ached, the back of her head felt rigid and hard and the rigidity reached to all her muscles, all her body quivered with spastic, retching sobs, her lungs groaned in the clamour for breath and tears. The family stopped eating and looked at her. It was Maura the eldest girl who took over.

'Come on Mam, come and lie down, I'll see to the rest of the meal. Come and have a little lie down.'

There was such a screaming in her brain, such an incredible inferno of noise and feeling, such a jumble of misery, surprise and grief that she wasn't really aware of Maura helping her into bed, of her shoes being eased off, of sheets being pulled up to her chin. Sound multiplied on sound, reverberation of bone-shaking, nerve destroying, throbbing, thudding and exploding. Noise thudded back from the inside of her skull, flung itself like living water from the walls of the room, enveloped muscle and fibre and cell in a sheet of tumult and catastrophe. Like hail against a window pane, like rocks tumbling down a mountain, like a bursting dam when the last

49

support has gone, her sobs grew in waves and cascades and subsided to grow higher, so that they flowed within and through and around her until the muscles of her feet ached with effort as much as the muscles of her face.

Unaccountably the sobbing ceased and she felt in herself such a sensation of limpid and untrammeled solitude, such an amazing unexperienced felicity, such a peacefulness of power and possibility that she had difficulty in associating the sensation with herself. She seemed to be floating in a warm and gentian sea, flat out upon the blue, below the blue above. Blue above and blue below, and she was warm and free, suspended between them, elemental, passive, powerful. Water stirred in supportive caress, lapping in soft undulations along her pliant limbs.

She stared up at the distant sky, white sea birds were etched far above her and behind them, an infinity. She felt as if the water beneath went as deep as the sky was high, and between them she was suspended in a serene lucent ether. Time was immaterial, she existed there for ever in glorious silence, just herself and the sea, and the quiet distant birds.

But it seemed in a while, as if she were no longer in the sea, or of the sea but walking beside it, walking without object or effort along a high cliff path. It was more as if she had become part of the sky and was attaining this incredible summit by floating through air, or swimming upwards, light and supported. Her path was bordered by tropical creepers, winding up withered trees, and like fountains releasing from their highest point cascades of scarlet blossoms. The flowers were like red stars, blood red and poised and separate. In that extraordinary light, the red was more remarkable than any seen before, a colour to be tasted and felt and smelled as well as seen, and the green was more green, the white more pure and all the colours and sensations were true and perfect beyond conception.

As she looked at that blue dazzling sea, she perceived that it was not, as she had supposed, empty but that surging up from its depths, rising and disappearing were numerous fishes, small red, fluorescent fishes. It was restful to watch them moving and darting. They formed accidental patterns, flitting about in small groups that split and reformed, sometimes one swimming off alone. They were like scattered petals, swimming garlands and posies, gathering around a dark spreadeagled body, floating face up to the sky. She knew it was Morrisey, his pose uncharacteristically relaxed. The fish swarmed round him, multiplying into shoals, hundreds and hundreds of small flashing mites. As she watched, one shoal in a body swooped towards his right hand. She watched them swim away, and the red dye spreading out in the blue. It was scarlet as the fishes at first but soon began to fade and dilute as it spread wider. Then there came another shoal, and a new red sea-cloud poured from the region of his neck. It seemed brighter and thicker, and fish and colour merged as in coloured smoke. The colour seemed to attract more fish because shoals were coming from every direction. More and more fronds of scarlet spiralled through the blue. The dark body had become obscure in the melee of red fishes and red blood.

There was a noise edging in on her total blissful silence. There was a rattle and a voice. Then the rattle was a thin clink and the voice approaching was saying,

'Mam, Mam, are you all right?'

Mrs. Morrisey shook off the mists of sleep clinging implacably around her. Rosaleen was standing with a cup of tea, looking with concern at the rock upon which she relied.

'Oh lovey, you woke me up' said Mrs. Morrisey 'And I was having such a beautiful dream.'

Word of Mouth Objector

Marie Hurley

THE BULLOCKS stood big and square. Their steaming breath gave off the odour of barley and rye grass hay as they marched carelessly, half watching the yard-cleaning activities, and eyeing the remaining ration of fodder in the stone trough.

Finbar, from his eerie on the barn, then tossed down yellow fluted bales of straw to his wife, who undid their bonds and watched them swell out like proven dough. They both shook out the bedding into the red corrugated iron shed, sealing it off from the greedy audience until later, when it would be fresh for their slumbers.

Two freckled children ran down the narrow passage and climbed up on the gate, feathers of hair askew, like baby lapwings.

'Mam, there's someone at the door looking for you.' The bigger girl announced this in a sing-song voice, full of self-importance. She then blinked widely as if to assure them that it wasn't about anything she did. 'It's a man', she finished flatly.

Phil looked up, her short curls caught for a minute in a frosty halo.

'Who is it?' The child knew most of the locals. Her nose and cheeks were pink as a Reubens' angel.

'You know, the man with the brown car', the small one sucked her thumb.

Her husband turned on the hose again. Nose deep in the rich molasses supplement, the prize friesians wallowed in the heavy tropical smell, and surfaced brown tipped, to gaze greasily over the farm gate. Like a circus team they moved their acquired green socks this way and that, as the brush followed its usual course along the washed concrete, and arranged their mud splattered bodies to feel the cold smile of the wintry sun.

'I won't be long Barry. Come on.' She caught the sticky little clutch of fingers in each hand and skipped them over stones.

For late April it had grown cold. The animals were going out on grass next day and would have to be dosed. Luckily the twenty acres was a heavy perfumed carpet of food, and the last two days sharpness would go as quickly as it had come.

A familiar Cortina was parked in the drive. The warble fly man looked down at the children fondly. 'Hello Mrs. Dillon', he said beaming. 'The vet asked me to call in passing to give you this package and to tell you that all the cows he tested are clear.'

'Will you sit down and have a cup of tea?' she asked automatically, knowing full well that he would, and be there for the next hour.

'God the prices are down something terrible at the marts' he droned and she began to drift . . . sometimes she felt she was just a breeding unit herself not understanding her connection with the world outside, great discoveries, turmoil, and conflict.

'Brennans are exporting calves now, a planeload went off yesterday to France. The prices are too high for the dry stock men and lining the pockets of the big dairy farmer.' She remembered being up all night with a difficult cow calving. The poor creature slipped on the wet boards and broke her pelvis. After that she made sure there was enough bedding underfoot. Lost one beautiful milker and a bull calf, so much for the beef men and their loss of sleep! ·

She listened. Small talk, the important social grooming. Sometimes she felt lonely within herself, for all the untouched springs of hope fading within her.

'Did ye put fertiliser out in the field?' He chewed with relish on a thick buttered slice of currant cake.

'No' she said, 'But it's fine. Isn't it?'

He licked the tip of his finger delicately.

'It's the best land this side of Limerick. Is Finbar about?'

'You'll find him down at the silo pit. I'd say he's feeding the cows now.'

He put on the cloth cap. 'I'll just drop down a minute. The sup of tea was grand. I'm obliged to you.'

She rose with her man and worked with him. Shared his life. But there was something else. A vague feeling of un-expressed needs. Men's desires and dreams were adequately chronicled, throughout the ages. Children clung to women. Perhaps with the pill, they could paint their own canvas, in the space between . . . the silence.

Deirdre and Tamala, out in the garden, threw fists of earth at each other, whooping and crying simultaneously. They were small but energetic and kept pushing her patience to see what they could get away with. Little adults. Beginning to manipulate us.

She knelt and smelled the primroses, laid the cool velvety petals against her skin.

Finbar walked towards her without calling, in his recent secretive way.

'What are you doing out here?' he was tall, with a slightly ruddy complexion, dusty corn hair, and blue eyes; her love, her life.

'I'm admiring the flowers.'

'Why don't you pick a few for the table?'

'You know I'd rather see them growing' she said. 'Anyway, they last longer this way. They're dead when cut.' He pulled her ear playfully.

'I'm going up to the North tomorrow with Bill. He's

54

bringing down a load. Will you manage?' So the tea and the chat wasn't without fruit.

'You won't be staying the night? she asked.

'No, we'll leave before dark. Get a room at the usual place . . . it's safer.'

They went into the large kitchen, and mixed the worm dose into a pink milky paste. In the absence of an injector gun, she rinsed out a plastic screw top tomato sauce container, with a nozzle. This was always a messy job, with the operator often more decorated than the animal safeguarded.

The cattle crush was a walled passage down which they walked to an enclosed pen. Each animal in turn had a pint of the bovine alka seltzer, before indulging himself in the bacchian delights of Dillon's pastures the next day.

'What time will you be leaving in the morning?' she asked eventually. These mysterious journeys made her uneasy.

'About nine. I'll be collecting Bill from the pub, he's borrowing Brennan's lorry.'

'Pigs is it?' She knew that there was a booming trade in pigs up and calves down the unapproved roads, for those with connections, or less brains than business sense.

'I told you that I want to see some breeders. Ask about a few milkers.' He always came back with a few quid extra. So much for high aspirations.

'I hope you're not doing anything risky, we have a good enough living as we are.' He looked worried. 'The milk is all we have until the price of stores goes up. If this summer is anything like the last, there'll be no feeding to keep any next winter. The only land making money now is building land. Ten cows won't feed us for the year.'

He looked in the mirror.

'I'll have a quick shave and pop down to see the lads, find out what prices they're making at Kilmallock Mart.

She walked out to the square yard, and sat on a painted bench. The evening was blistering and separating into night. Busy robins like exclamation marks arranged themselves carefully on trees. She was an unidentified substance. She was life. Shaped to convenience, but alive, responsive. She had let her house and children grow around her like protective clothing. Had become fragile and thin in spirit, untested in courage.

Later, as they lay there, entwined, her man felt warm and apricot sweet, that night, strange yet familiar.

At seven the alarm went off. The bed steamed pleasantly in the sharp black morning. Sleep hung stickily about her hair and eyelids. The dark shape under the covers purred like a trombone. Substance and images were all mixed up.

Outside the cows were a study in black and white. They stood quietly chewing like old philosophers, as Finbar attached the cups of the portable milking machine to each bovine dispenser, and whistled a little Elgar into appreciative ears.

They ate breakfast in silence, both reading different parts of the newspaper. 'Another soldier killed in Belfast' she read aloud. 'I wonder if he had a soul.' He looked up.

'I'll be going' he said as he kissed her lightly on the lips. 'I told Tom to drop up to give you a hand. If I'm held up I'll give you a ring.'

She watched him out to the old Peugeot, start up, and wave as he drove off. Deirdre had tiptoed into the kitchen, opened a large sweet tin now filled with sugar, and systematically removed each granule, spoonful by spoonful. The sugar bowl and table was glittering with its sticky mountain. Tamala who had followed downstairs as quietly as a kitten, was investigating the coal bucket.

Tom arrived on a motorbike. He was a pleasant youth who worked on the farm down the hill, and helped her out when they were busy.

'Turning out nice today' he volunteered as they made their way to the shed. The cloudless sky might be a good omen. She thought of the men in the lorry, trundling up to the unknown.

The cows had the peaky dry look humans acquire after a long time indoors. They were herded out from their cosy nest of six months, along the bridle path up to the pasture. The sheepdog tailed excitedly, keeping stragglers in check, until the gate was opened, and, cautious first, they bounded in gratefully, skipping and frolicking as gracefully as any square-legged 500 kilogram bovine can.

'There was a huge crowd in the bar last night. Padge Mahony was telling Bill that he'll be caught, one night, and it won't be for pigs either.' Tom was talking away, ignorant of the atmosphere. 'When Finbar came in, they started singing *The Patriot Game.*' Her face stopped him.

'They were only joking of course. Barry told them so many dealers are going up that they were bumper to bumper, and that they were contributing privately to build a flyover. He's always kidding them', he finished lamely. The boy went home but his words hung on. If they left before dark they'd be staying in Dundalk overnight. What was the name of the hotel again? She fiddled with the drawer in the hall table.

Her feelings of solidarity with the Provos were long gone. Like all power-mad organisations, she thought, they made decisions, personal decisions about the fate of many, without care or consultation. The only martyrs now, were victims. Did they hide in the undergrowth ready to pounce on the word-of-mouth objector? Or did they mix freely with like-minded casualties, nursing forever the unattended, unreachable sore of past history?

'Coward . . . I'm no coward' she once told an accuser. Less than you who support them from a safe distance. I've seen mistakes being made, people were shot in error. They destroy the body to kill the disease. We huddle together under the mantle of union disruption, church conservatism, and say let's pretend we are worried about the deaths. We are liars.

She scattered some grain for the hens watching them flutter, Burnt Sienna and Yellow Ochre, as they pecked in their domestic pen unable to really fly anymore, maybe not caring, possibly regretting in some undefined way what they exchanged for security.

She didn't want men to fight her wars for her. She didn't want their young beautiful bodies opened like valves on the roadside. She couldn't, nobody could afford the wisdom which they contained to be lost. There was a blurred line between respectful disagreement and challenge. She knew friendly articulate men who would go out at night and change into slobbering drunks or raging brutes, as if their lives were untrue. Perhaps unable to reach some patriarchial *ideal* of fleshless pleasure, any fall from grace was turned into a *grotesquerie*. The innocent drink, the woman, the snarling challenger, was caricatured, the soft friction lost.

There was a knock at the back door. Nora, Bill's wife delivered the car. She was small and sturdy, contained within herself. She could explore with words, once, and now was reduced to monosyllables.

They both finished boarding school together. Nora, articulate with the thought of becoming a journalist. She completed training at secretarial college which was all they had then and by perseverance started the long slow climb up the rungs of the splendid if unspectacular local paper. As her star started to shine she met Bill, and it seems they both were dazzled, because after her marriage, she always referred to her career as if it had reached its natural climax, and petered out.

'When is Francis starting school?' She had four children and the youngest was now about to be launched into the world.

'Next September', came the answer. 'I can't say I'll mind, she is beginning to become a handful.'

There was no harm in trying once more. 'Why don't you try submitting the odd article to the paper again. You'll have more time now that they are all at school.'

'Ah . . . no. I'm out of touch. I'll be feeding calves anyway.' Excuses. We'd run anywhere to avoid facing up to our limitations. Better not try. It might devastate us. Men have to do it daily.

Nora was rattling on, 'When I see the standard of writing now, and the work the women graduates are doing, a convent educated Sacred Heart Messenger standard of English housewife like myself wouldn't have a chance.'

The talk went back to Bill. 'Do you worry about him going up there so often?'

She lit a cigarette. 'He enjoys it, it's his life.' She debated on whether to relate Tom's story, and decided against it.

'I'm doing a bit of pottery . . .'

The women talked and at length she drove the visitor home, collecting the children from school on the way. The sky got dark. The rest of the day used her, and tired she collapsed in front of the television. Wars and rumours of wars. People like her, millions of them were doing nothing about it, sitting stupidly, wiped out with living. She switched off the set and put on some music, Dvorak. The 'phone rang. She jumped.

'Hello?' It was Bill.

'Where's Finbar?'

'Police station . . . being questioned.' He wasn't very coherent.

'What?'

The voice was far away.

'Now don't worry. I've only just been released. They won't charge him with anything.'

He sounded drunk.

'Can I ring him?'

'No, wait until the morning.'

This had happened before. To others. Well surely he was safe there? She tried not to think about it. He wasn't a criminal. Tom's words kept surfacing. He didn't do anything . . . did he? She remembered all she had read about imprisonment without trial. She made some coffee and put a dash of whiskey in it. Was he being tortured? That was ridiculous. They didn't do those things anymore. That was all done away with. Psychological terror they called it. She rang Nora.

'Oh don't worry' the breezy voice was unconcerned. 'Those piss arses have nothing else to do but question people.'

She went to bed feeling helpless. Drops fell against the window. She said an unaccustomed prayer for him. Rain pumped down all night. The house smelt of emptiness. She dozed and turned in the cold bed restless with fears of narrow roads, ambushes and sleazy motels with 'H Block' in neon lights, unwelcoming.

At six forty-five she dressed. She made a large bowl of porridge and left it to simmer on the black pewter range. She rang the station. No reply.

'Bastards!'

The cows had to be milked, so she clanked the feed bucket and they trailed in like weary mountaineers, after a hard climb, sated with spring grass. Milking them relaxed her, and she hummed a little étude from Chópin, for their selection that day.

'. . . bomb blast kills three' the radio announced unhelpfully, at eight o'clock. 'Soldier wounded.'

The creamery lorry would be arriving soon. She looked up the checklist of milk supplied, and scribbled in today's figures. The aluminium container would have to be boiled and sterilised later. One of the cows had slight mastitis. She'd have to be treated with antibiotic and her milk thrown out until it was cleared.

She tried to concentrate. Bills for the ESB overdue. The creamery would have to pay her, first. Only for the cows she would have no weekly income, and now, one was out. School books and clothes were so expensive. I'll buy a sewing machine if I sell enough pots she thought. The local store had promised to stock some during the summer.

She rang again.

'No' the dark voice hedged, 'I'm afraid we have absolutely no information. What is your number?' She quietly replaced the receiver.

The children had to be brought to school. 'Will Daddy bring me a present?' Tamala asked coyly.

'Yes darling.' It sounded reassuring.

Tom was there when she arrived back.

'I heard they were caught' he muttered sympathetically, in his tactless fashion. 'They were bringing calves down, it's nothing.'

She wished he'd not be so dramatic.

'The town has it that it was gelignite and that they were carting it up.' He had it said before he could see the horror it implied.

'That's pure invention' she answered succinctly, handing him the tube of ointment.

'Will you put that on Matilda, she's in the barn, leave her tethered or she'll knock my pottery.' Her body felt cold and detached.

Gelignite! He wouldn't be such a fool. She went down to the field to check that the water tank was working and was clean.

Bringing up pigs along the unapproved roads was big business. Everyone knew that. There was a small profit in it, as they loaded up with the cheaper Northern calves which had been compulsorily ear tagged. A drink at the pub near Forkhill, back over the border hopefully safely, remove the tags, dust off the ears, and sell them to farmers in the next trip up at five pounds a time, to put on their own cattle, the dodgy ones. All this for maybe a bullet in the head. Bill thought it worth his time, so why was Finbar held?

She couldn't ring the garda station. Not yet. It was too uncertain. Tom helped her to milk the cows again at five and told her about a cousin of a friend of his, who was taken away, out of his car by the gunmen . . . and never seen again. Mr. Dillon's lucky . . . you know. It could be worse. He had the bit between his teeth.

She rang twice again, and was asked more questions, referred to other departments. She slammed the mouthpiece angrily on the 'rest'.

Deirdre started to whine. 'I don't want to go to bed until Daddy comes back.' She got a blanket and all three curled up on the settee, nodding with exhaustion. At half past ten the front door opened. She clutched them stiffly.

'Phil' the familiar voice reached her. He entered the room, unshaven and weary.

'Oh love,' she hugged him tightly, protectively, her family restored to her again.

'Bill dropped me off . . . I'm very tired, we were driving for seven hours. I had no sleep last night.

He slumped in the armchair. She was crying, then the children started.

'Oh come on now. It wasn't all that bad.' He ruffled her hair. 'After all I was where I shouldn't have been.' He tickled the child's chin. 'The pigs are being held as evidence.' Tamala bawled.

'Imagine they are all behind bars with striped pyjamas on, honking in Irish.' The child giggled.

'I don't know how those stupid bastards were not run out of the country long ago' she said.

THESE NEEDLES THROUGH OUR OWN LIVES, TOO, HAVE MOVED

Joyce McGreevy Stafford

In the Musee de Cluny we toured the famous chamber,
Taking in the tapestries of creatures now extinct:
The unicorn and its lady, a pale, complacent lady,
The stitches of her smile turned all but indistinct.

These needles through our own lives, too, have moved;
Feminine fingers have prodded, bloodied the thread,
Staining the soft silver a violent red.
What matter, however, when they will only hang,
Hurtful to no one's eyes, on the wrong side?

Only in the Museum of Dreams do we
Come to visit this underside of our lives:
The tangled threads, unwoven, wild, uncut.
Yet even there we act unmoved, admit
To no terror, knowing we need not linger;
Like the needle returning forever, we never linger.

DENIAL

Elizabeth A. O'Brien

Green, liquid cold, smacking and
                    sucking
The solid harbour wall.
How I wanted to drink . . . free! oh loose and free!
Clean me, clear me, bathe
My whole self.
You summer sea!
Here, tamed to man's limit — protesting and beautiful.
Beyond — you natural wild free life.
You are fresh and strikingly blue with the sun.
And pound and crash
And caress — majestic full white!
Gleaming vigorous white and glorious gold-and-blue —
Shouting and glad together.
Powerful!
And gentle light sky and mellow and peacefully content.

I want to kick off my warm close plimsoles —
— Pulled tight —
Sweaty and soft. Thick socks and
Roll up my jeans and
Let my toes and white stale feet and exposed creased legs . . .
S t r e t c h . . . and . . . breathe.
And walk in the cold sand of the near beach
Oh natural and naked!

And the effervescent white blue of the t

                    um

                          Splashing

                 bl

                 ing

Waters! Rushing to me
Caressing and shocking and refreshing.
Now live pulsing feet and pulsing heart
And rolling waves
Drinking in the sun and melting to

                   liquid

                     green

                         transparency

As they soar and stretch . . .
Then, intoxicated
Surging and smashing into breathless splintering of
Gleaming vigorous blue-white-and-gold!
How I wanted to swim and dive in your laughter
And melt into your life.
How I yearned to — my heart cried out to you.
BUT
Man's timekeeper strapped to my wrist

                   Weighed

                    on my mind.

That such a tiny self-assured line —
irritating incessant marker of time
should steal my thoughts and

                avert my gaze.

This virgin view — this virgin life does not know of time.
I could not touch it. Join. Give my whole self.
My head was turned reluctantly up at the
Grey dry road.
The bus will be here any minute now.

SHOP ASSISTANTS RULE NOT OK

Mary Reilly

The cash register tings busily,
Electronic wizardry designed to shock,
Mistakes can be costly;
Two thousand pounds for ten pairs of socks!

The money ebbs and flows,
Hand to hand, purse to till.
Paper in exchange for food and clothes.

Will this fit a man with a beer belly?
Will that suit a boy with red hair?
Will this sag while constantly sitting in front
of the telly?

I'm not a man, I really don't know.
But you work here, please help me!
A fixed smile, why do I feel so low?

SLOUGHING OFF

Ivy Bannister ·

Split; tear; be warned; take care.
Having drunk your kisses
And your blond brother's too

My bruised flesh swells,
A misbegotten fruit.
The purpled skin splits.

With an analytic eye he notes
The jagged rent between my breasts,
Observes the skin peel back,

Layer exposing raw layer.
Do they make him smile,
Those white dead bits flaking,

Wafting slowly to the floor
Like tiny, bleeding petals?
Ache, ache, I grow, I groan.

New shocks jolt old mythologies.
I cast off stale friends, stale scenes.
Fertilised by negatives,

The corrupt egg shall be rooted from the womb.
Will I father my own child?
I spit out dead thoughts, rotten dreams.

My limbs squirm like an eel pit;
My arms burst, my thighs heave.
Crawling forth agonised from

A tattered, battered skin,
I give birth to myself.
Be warned; take care; I split; I tear.

Poor Dear Neighbour

Patricia Boyne

I REALLY can't imagine why poor, dear Mrs. Brady should have behaved so shabbily. After all, I was her nearest neighbour — just over the garden wall, you might say. I know she liked me; at least, I feel sure she did. Why, she had no one of her own class nearby, no one really educated, so to speak. She enjoyed our little chats, too. That's why I made every excuse I could to knock at her door and try to take her out of herself. Many's the day I went along and asked for a loan of an egg, even though I had a couple at home in the fridge. Or, I pretended that the vacuum was out of order, and called to borrow hers. You see, I had to have an excuse for calling; she was so shy, so retiring, almost a recluse, in fact. That was really the root of the trouble; she was too much alone, kept too much to herself. No wonder her poor brain snapped, at last.

Not that she's in a mental home or anything like that. Not that I *know* of, at any rate. Of course, I haven't heard any news of the Bradys since they left Ivy Villas. Maybe that's what happened; maybe she *was* put into somewhere for a rest cure. I shouldn't wonder if that's the reason she disappeared so very mysteriously.

Yes, her husband got a transfer to somewhere else. That was the story. He is a civil servant, though anyone less civil it would be hard to imagine. It must have taken some weeks to arrange the transfer. Funny that she never even mentioned it to me. Just disappeared overnight. I never took to Mr. Brady. Not that I spoke much with him — not after that first Saturday in the garden when he was so rude to me. There he was, digging away like a beaver when I popped my head over the wall, wondering what they intended to plant. The Smiths who had the house before the Bradys never put anything down, year in year out, except some potatoes and cabbages, and an odd row of lettuce. There were a few fruit bushes there already. Not that Mollie Smith bothered her head to make jam, that big lazy creature with her brood of children running wild. The Smiths stayed about three years. Odd, the way next door keeps changing tenants. One would imagine that with houses so scarce people would be glad to settle down in comfort, semi-detached, three bedrooms, a good-sized kitchen, two receptions, bathroom, etc. and all beside a friendly neighbour.

Perhaps not having a family makes Harry and me so settled. Of course, I would have liked a couple of kids, to share my loneliness, for it *is* lonely with Harry away all the week and only the daily help for company. Lucky she's such a bright girl and keeps me right up-to-the-minute in all the local happenings. Harry's a rep. for industrial boilers, you know, and has to keep on the move. Makes plenty of money, but we're not a bit purse proud. He likes to see me well turned out, of course. Mrs. Brady has no taste at all about clothes. I did my best, very tactfully, but she just hasn't it in her.

To get back to Mr. Brady in the garden. Would you believe it? He hardly lifted his eyes to salute me. I said very sweetly, 'Won't you bring Mrs. Brady in some Saturday evening for cards and a chat?' Looking well past me, he growled out: 'We detest both.' Mrs. Brady explained later, during one of our cosy chats that Mr. Brady was not really of a social disposition and had a positive hatred of small talk. I *do* believe he had

71

something to hide, though I didn't find out just what. Perhaps it was only a strange kink. No wonder poor Mrs. Brady got a bit odd, living with a crank like that. The nerve of him, having airs and graces on a salary of under five thousand a year. I found that out, by the way, just after they came here. I remember mentioning this very matter of salary to Nellie Marron at the bazaar last summer, and asking her how the Bradys managed. She looked at me very queerly. But she's an odd bod; these women careerists often are, sort of frustrated, don't you think? One hesitates to call them vicious, but they can make plenty of trouble. I didn't know at the time that she was so friendly with Mrs. Brady. Oh, well, 'birds of a feather . . . .'

Yes, Mrs. Brady had one child, a little girl called Annie. An old-fashioned name that suited the child to perfection. She's small and slight, stunted, one might almost say, and very shy. Or is it sly? I could never decide which. She's supposed to be very clever. Only a few months ago, I heard about Annie Brady getting first place in the secondary school scholarships. Little Jean Wilson told me, for when I was on my way to the sewing guild, Jean was coming home from school, and I stopped her to find out whether the new baby had come. It hadn't, but it was near at hand. Jean told me about the school, and about Annie getting first place. I turned right back on my tracks, to be the first with the good news to Mrs. Brady. She *was* pleased. But I thought she'd bring me in for a cup of tea and a chat, instead of keeping me on the doorstep and mumbling some excuse about her daily not having come and that she was baking in the kitchen. Naturally, I volunteered to forget the sewing for once and help in the kitchen. But she sort of tightened up and said thanks, but she'd manage all right, and Mr. Brady would be home early. What a reception for a bearer of good news!

'Aren't you glad about Annie?' I asked.

'Delighted,' she smiled, a little artificially, I thought. But then, she had a bad smile; I told her several times not to smile when having a photo taken; her teeth were crooked.

'Fancy that little girl being so clever,' I remarked. 'And she

72

looks so frail, so delicate.'

'Oh, Annie's a hardy child,' she replied.

She knew I always sympathised with her about Annie being underweight and skinny. There's an old saying I often quoted to her. 'Nay chiel is better'n aye chiel.'

Maybe she didn't like that remark of mine about Annie. Truth hurts, you know. But surely it's better not to live in a fog of false fantasies. That's what I always say to Harry. Not that he's at home much. You'd think that after being away the whole week he'd like to dig his heels in at home for the weekend. Not a bit of it. Out golfing Saturday afternoon and all Sunday — except for the occasional hour or two he spends looking after his precious vegetable marrows, the only things he cares for in the garden. Off on the road again first thing Monday morning.

How old was Mrs. Brady? I never found out, for certain. Though I gave her plenty of chances to confide. But Nellie Marron's young sister was at school with Mrs. Brady, and I reckon, counting things up, they're both in the mid-forties. Nellie herself is forty-nine. A dangerous age. Not that all ages aren't dangerous, but the mid-forties are particularly so. Perhaps that's what caused Mrs. Brady to behave so very strangely to me immediately before they left Ivy Villas. It's said that people can turn on their nearest and dearest at a time like that. For she really liked me, I believe. She used to say: 'How kind of you to call, Mrs. Greene.' True, I rarely got past the front door; she was always so busy. That daily of hers, whenever the slattern *did* arrive for a day's work seemed more of a hindrance than a help. But then, poor Mrs. Brady never had any system; no planning, no efficiency. A house just doesn't run itself on such random lines, does it?

Oh, indeed, that *was* a most mysterious illness of Mrs. Bradys just before she left Ivy Villas. I knew she was ill, of course; the doctor called every morning — not *my* doctor, though I *did* have Mrs. Brady's up some time ago. I had to change to another doctor; he (Mrs. Brady's doctor, that is) started to look at me in a supercilious way, almost like a sneer, I felt. But Harry says I'm far too sensitive, that I feel a slight where none is intended. Doctors grow strange as they get older, I think. With all the pressure of work and all the abnormal cases they handle. Well, as I say, I saw his car outside Brady's every morning and Mrs. Brady didn't appear either back or front, so I guessed she was ill. It was my duty to help out. I made a delicious bowl of beef tea, put it into a warmed enamel can and went next door. The daily opened the door, that churlish girl. I meant to take the beef tea upstairs to Mrs. Brady myself. Would you credit it? That stupid girl barred the way, wouldn't let me pass.

'Mrs. Brady is asleep now,' she said. 'Doctor's orders that she be left sleeping.' What state must the poor woman's room be in, left to the mercies of that silly slattern? If only I could have got up, I would have straightened things out and made her comfortable. I called a few more times, only to be met with 'Mrs. Brady is sleeping, Ma'am.'

That was the turning point. A few days later I saw Mrs. Brady cutting a cabbage in her back garden. Naturally, I popped my head over the wall and called a cheery 'Good morning'. Her lack of response should have warned me that she was not herself yet. But I was determined to cheer her up. I asked if she meant to divide her carnations this year and what kind of border she intended to put around the big bed next spring. Then I went on to ask her how she felt. She said she was quite better, adding that it had been 'just a chill'. Fancy telling *me* that fib! I ask you! I said with real concern: 'My dear, I hope you haven't been taking too many sleeping pills.' Then the horrid thing happened. I had just rested an extra large veg-marrow, one of Harry's biggest, on the wall, as I was going to make jam for the parish sale. And I wanted Mrs. Brady to see how fine a specimen it was. But before I had time to say anything about it, Mrs. Brady came over to the wall, looked fiercely at the marrow and said passionately (I can feel the vibrations even now): 'I hate it. I hate it. It's face reminds me of someone I know, someone rude and dull and stupid, someone pushing and intruding.' Then she laughed into my face and plunged her sharp knife right into the marrow, before she ran back into her house.

Looking back at the incident, I can see now that it was definitely a brainstorm. At the time, I was too flabbergasted to do anything but gape after her.

The very next morning, the Bradys went away. I was awakened by a car grinding its brakes to a stop outside their front window, and when I hopped out of bed and hurried to my window I saw Mr. and Mrs. Brady and Annie come out through their gate and into the waiting car. I tapped at the bedroom window, but they didn't seem to hear. I wondered where they were going at that hour of the morning. Some time later, a big furniture van arrived and the men started carrying things out. I called at the door to see whether I could help in any way, and that stupid girl was in charge. She said she didn't know anything only that the Bradys had gone to another house. The men were very rude, too, pretending not to hear my questions. I saw all the stuff, of course, very ordinary, rather dull and heavy, not like the new shiny stuff I have in all the rooms. But poor Mrs. Brady must have regretted her behaviour the day before, for she left me a little momento, a souvenir of our friendship. The girl gave it to me in a small box. It was a brass ornament that used to stand on a bracket in their hall, three funny monkeys with a motto underneath, 'See no evil, hear no evil, speak no evil.' It's not the kind of piece that appeals to me. But it may be an antique. There it is, on the shelf over your head.

I'm sorry she grew so odd. We could have been good friends. Who's living next door, now? Well, nobody yet. But they're due to move in next week. A newly-married couple. I heard something about them. She's over thirty; a bit settled for a bride. But she'll be company for me. I have a feeling that we're going to be friends.

Death
is a Dream

Honor Duff

DOROTHY DROVE her Mercedes up the driveway to the Old People's Home with what her sister-in-law thought was unseemly haste.

'You'd better slow down,' she warned, watching the pebbles spurt from under the wheels to land on the neat grass verge lined with daffodils.

'I mean, some of the residents might be out walking.'

Dorothy sighed but kept up the pace until they turned the last bend, slowing only as the large grey house flanked by pillars, came into sight.

'Claire,' she said then with forced patience, 'if you had any professional knowledge of how these places are run you'd know that the residents are not allowed to meander up and down this driveway; it would put both themselves and car drivers at risk. There are plenty of secluded walks for them within the grounds.'

'It sounds like a prison,' Claire said bitterly and looked sympathetically towards Mrs. Boyd, her mother-in-law, but the old lady patted Claire's hand and said in placatory tones, 'The grounds look very nice, dear, all those flowers and trees.'

Dorothy braked sharply in front of the house and ordered her ten year old son, Anthony to help his grandmother out of the car, glancing at his bent head as she did so. Both he and his Aunt Claire had behaved all the way out as if they were going to a hanging, and her mother's obvious striving to be bright and cheerful had increased her annoyance. She lifted her mother's suitcase from the boot and banged it on the gravel.

Mrs. Boyd was staring across the lawn, one hand leaning on the shoulder of young Anthony, and Claire had linked her other arm tightly.

'I hope those trees aren't Dutch Elms, Gran,' Anthony said worriedly, 'because if they are they might have that disease and have to be chopped down.'

Mrs. Boyd laughed, 'I hope that won't happen, love, but they seem like healthy enough specimens at this distance anyway', which was more, she thought privately, than you could say for the few elderly people sitting on white painted benches under the trees, or walking slowly in twos on a small path bordering the other side of the lawn. They had a kind of general frailty about them, and their movements seemed deliberate and premeditated. I am one of them, she thought with a kind of shock, even as her mind rejected the idea, I am one of them.

Dorothy strode ahead with the suitcase, a tall determined looking woman with closely waved brown hair and a face that would have been handsome but for a rather Roman nose. She felt ill-served by her whole family. Her brother Ben, Claire's husband, had not even made a point of coming today to show support for the idea. Her own husband Noel, was of course excused on the grounds of business engagements, and at least she knew she had his full support. He had even agreed that it would be no harm to make Tony stand on his feet and not cling so childishly to his grandmother. Such an emotional attachment to an elderly female was unhealthy in a boy of his age.

She had told Noel some weeks previously, over a couple of much-needed gin and tonics at the end of a hard day, about Ben and Claire's ridiculous idea that her mother should go to live with them permanently.

'As if,' she said savagely, 'a woman who has had two heart attacks could survive even a full day in that mad house with all those undisciplined children.'

Noel had agreed it was a crazy idea, but then surprised her by suggesting that they take Mrs. Boyd themselves, permanently.

'I mean, she's no trouble when she stays weekends' he had said, but Dorothy had pointed out, reasonably and with logic that weekends were different to working weeks when the house was deserted all day, and Tony at Boarding school. As a doctor she had to think of her mother's physical and psychological needs at the same time, and she did not think it would be either desirable or economically practical to hire a nurse or daily companion for the old lady. She could not continue to live alone, that was for sure, even with the helpful neighbours she had.

Claire and Ben had both shot down the idea of the Home, talking irrationally and over-dramatically of poorhouses and almshouses, as if the chosen place was not the very best, most exclusive and expensive in County Dublin.

'It's natural for a grandparent to live under the same roof as her family' Claire had argued. 'Look at Spain, you always see lots of grannies minding the children all day and coming to the beach for picnics; they don't shove their old people into institutions.'

'I hardly think that two weeks in Torremolinos qualifies you to have a deep knowledge of Spanish family structures, Claire,' Dorothy had said icily, 'and in any event, what we are discussing here is a sick woman who needs to be where she can get rapid care and attention when necessary.'

Yes, it had been an uphill struggle with herself emerging as the villain of the piece. They did not seem to realise just how much influence had been needed to get her mother at the head of a long queue. She told the others to wait now while she went into the office. They stood in the carpeted hallway, looking around at the chintz-covered furniture, and the tables full of magazines and spring flowers until Dorothy returned with Mrs. Warren who, together with her husband, ran the home.

They followed the woman up the carpeted stairway to a pleasant room looking out on the grounds. Through the trees you could see a glimpse of sea and a small piece of Dalkey Island. She was a cheerful, middle-aged woman, a trained nurse, and had that slight hardness of manner that long years of dealing with sick people brings. She opened cupboards and a wardrobe, tested the central heating, wished Mrs. Boyd a happy stay with them and said she would send up afternoon tea.

Mrs. Boyd suddenly wished there were nuns, quiet dedicated women who loved the wounded Christ in people and to whom she could talk about death. Her room was clinically neat except for a vase of roses on the bedside table, some of whose petals had fallen on the polished surface.

'Roses in April', she said wonderingly, 'they'll be hothouse, I suppose.' On top of a cupboard was a large, cellophane-wrapped bouquet of Spring flowers, tulips, daffodils and irises with a card from the family. Around this were ranged several cards showing black cats, horseshoes, houses with chimneys, spelling out such words as 'Good Luck', or 'Every Happiness in your New Home'.

Mrs. Boyd exclaimed over the flowers and the cards and while Dorothy unpacked her suitcase and put her things away, she unwrapped the flowers and held them out to Tony to smell.

'There's no smell at all, Gran,' he said disappointedly, 'I can only get that other smell, it's all over this place and in this room too.'

'Anthony!' Dorothy turned from her arranging, snatched the flowers from her mother and placed them symmetrically in a vase which she filled from the small adjoining bathroom.

'There is no smell at all,' she told her son, 'you are imagining it.'

Tony turned to the window and looked out, 'There is,' he muttered under his breath. His grandmother stroked his head and told him:

'You know, pet, when people get old they begin to go off a bit the same as flowers or food or trees in the autumn. You know the smell you get from dead leaves?' He nodded, 'Well,' she continued, 'that's only a sign of new life, young things growing.' She kissed his upturned face, 'you smell of daisies and clover yourself'. There was anguish in the thought that she would see very little of this beloved child or his small cousins. She needed to see and touch their rounded limbs, watch their clear eyes and fresh mouths, all affirmations of renewal.

A smiling girl came in with a loaded tea-tray and they poured and drank and chatted superficially, Dorothy slipping out after a few minutes for a professional chat with Mrs. Warren. When she returned, they prepared to leave. Dorothy admonished her mother about taking tablets, resting and eating properly, gave her a brief kiss and left abruptly. Tony and Claire both wept, clinging to her until she too cried a little before shooing them away.

She watched the car draw away, the scrunch of gravel reminding her of her boarding school days; the hollow feeling in your stomach when you were deposited, and the happiness of watching for her father's old Ford ploughing furrows through the convent pebbles at end of term.

Prowling around the room, she examined its strangeness like a cat transferred to unfamiliar surroundings. And as buttering a cat's paws is supposed to make it stay in a new home, so had her family done some paw-buttering in the shape of a new transistor, a colour TV and a pretty tea set for entertaining.

The radio was nice, but she wished she had something to play her old records on. She hadn't dared to put them on Dorothy and Noel's expensive stereo equipment. Claire was minding them for her, promising to keep them well out of the reach of the children. They were all the old songs she and Ned had loved — John McCormack, Richard Tauber, Paul Robeson . . . Ned used to sing 'Macushla' to her, he had a nice voice, much in demand at parties. Nobody sang at parties any more, or played the piano. It was all that peculiar music that had no recognisable melody.

She moved to the window and looked at the small bit of the island in the distance. She and Ned had rowed over there often and picnicked on the springy grass.

'When I retire,' he used to say, 'we'll move permanently to a small island, just the two of us.'

Her eyes filled with sudden tears and she tried to fight off the sharp longing and loneliness for him which, she felt sure, would increase in this place.

'Macushla, Macushla your red lips are saying that death is a dream, and that love is for ever . . . ' she whispered. There was a knock on the door and the girl came in to collect the tray.

'Mrs. Warren says you might like to come downstairs and meet some of the other residents' she said pleasantly. It was an order rather than a suggestion, and Mrs. Boyd obeyed.

The first week fell into its own pattern, and as in her memories of schooldays, the hours were ruled by bells. There was the tonk-tonk-tonk of the nearby church bell, the silvery tinkle of the meal bell and the electronic chimes of the hall door bell. If hearts were like bells, she thought, her own must sound tinny and unmelodious, with a lead clapper encased in thin metal. She did not think she was likely to start any friendships. The other residents were pleasant enough, and she swopped the small change of daily life with them gladly, but her few remaining old friends could not be expected to make the long journey to see her except occasionally. Her generation of women were not, in general, car drivers, and one of them, Lil, had been really exhausted after taking two buses to reach the Home. But it didn't matter in the final analysis because she had a strange certainty that her stay here would be a very brief one. Yet her longing to join Ned was tinged with dread ever since she had spoken to Father Justin, Dorothy and Noel's priest friend.

Father Justin was well known on TV. He had a beautiful head of wavy silver hair and a sonorous voice. He smoked Turkish cigarettes in an ebony holder and had written many books on controversial Church topics. That was all Mrs. Boyd knew about him, and she had mistakenly, one night in

Dorothy's drawing room asked him about married people meeting after death.

The priest had spoken humorously as if she were a little girl, now too old to believe in Santa Claus or fairies. She watched the ash grow long on his cigarette and when he tapped it into the ashtray with a manicured finger, she could feel the dust of it on her tongue and lips. His log had fallen like stones into the pool of her peace, sending ripples of doubt and anxiety through her whole being even as she tried to tell herself that even such a clever man as he could not know for sure.

Mrs. Warren provided ministers for whatever religions were there to be catered to. The Catholics, who were in the minority, had Father Murtagh. He was an unruly looking young man with badly-cut black hair and an equally badly cut soutane which swung to across a pair of scuffed boots. Strange to see such a young priest wearing such conventional clothes, she thought. At the end of her first week, he said Mass that Sunday in the television lounge. As it was the Easter season he spoke of death and resurrection, the empty tomb and Mary Magdalen's tears. Death was only a gateway, he told them, a gateway leading to our beloved dead. Father Justin's ironic words interposed themselves on the young priest's sentences and Mrs. Boyd tried to blot them out by carefully concentrating on the sermon. He was saying the last two lines of John Donne's poem on Death; Donne, he told them, like Mary Magdalen, had been a great sinner and a great lover and in admonishing Death to 'be not proud', he also affirmed.

'One short sleep past, we wake eternally,
 And death shall be no more, Death thou shalt die.'

Wasn't that a comforting thought, he asked the rows of old faces watching him, 'Death *thou* shalt die', he waited for a few minutes then added, 'He was dead right'. There were a few polite laughs at the weak joke and the young priest smiled and continued:

'You know, some people say we won't meet our loved ones in Heaven, or won't be to them as we were on earth. Well now, I don't believe that at all. I know that after I look on the face of God I'll see my parents as I used to see them in the kitchen at home. She'll be kneading bread and he'll be smoking his pipe at the range. It'll be a homecoming. My mother'll wipe the flour off her hands and we'll hug each other and my father will jump up and tell her to call in all the neighbours for a hooley. We'll push back the furniture, he'll play his accordion and we'll dance and dance until the streets of Heaven ring with the sound of our joy at being together again.'

Mrs. Boyd dropped her face into her hands as the blessed cleansing tears ran through her fingers. That young man with his shrunken robe and dusty boots had told her what she wanted to hear. For the first time in weeks she slept that night without feeling she was laying her head on a pillow of dust.

The next day was clear and lovely, blue sky and young buds and birds carolling in the garden. She felt excited and lively as if anticipating something good. The grounds seemed small and confining on such a day and with great daring and a few cautionary glances backwards she slipped out through a little-used door in the wall running along a quiet back lane.

She started to go down towards the harbour, but then remembered a favourite spot where she used to go with Ned years and years ago. She hesitated a moment, remembering that it involved a climb up a steep hill and then a treacherous walk down rock-hewn steps to a little sandy inlet. However, possessed as she was of a strange new recklessness, a sort of truant schoolgirl mischieviousness, she set off, stopping now and then to rest against sun-warmed walls, and pat some friendly dogs out for their own morning strolls. Coming at last to the chosen spot she noticed with a stab of disappointment that the approach to the inlet was now a park with trim flower beds and wooden seats placed at regular intervals. But the inlet was still there, far below and seemingly unchanged.

Grasping the handrail at the top of the steps, she made her way down, feeling slightly dizzy and wishing for Ned's hand under her elbow. However, at the bottom, she was rewarded by the sight of the little cove as they had known it. A shining expanse of silvery-green sea grass backed onto the walled garden of a house above, while below, the water lapped in and out of a half-moon of fine sand. A huge moss-covered rock rose from the water's edge, and this too, she remembered, leaning gratefully against its bulk and fingering the saffron and grey lichen growing in patches on it.

It had been a long walk and climb and she felt very tired suddenly. A seagull flew onto the top of the nearby wall and regarded her with wicked yellow eyes. Her children used to feed a pet seagull at home, calling him Dick and delighting in the way he gulped down huge lumps of food and gabbled for more. A blackbird flew out of the garden with something in its beak, and to her dismay, the gull zoomed in on it like a dive bomber. The two bodies, black and white, tangled in mid-air and then fell out of sight behind the rock. Mrs. Boyd waited and listened but heard nothing. The gull had probably pecked the blackbird to death. She tried to go around the rock by way of the sea but the water was too deep and it would take her ages to remove shoes and stockings. She started, instead to climb the lower part of the rock where it sloped towards the garden wall. About half-way, the blackbird flew up suddenly, startling her with a shrill cry but seeming un-harmed except for the loss of a few feathers, one of which floated down to the sand. It disappeared into the green safeness of the garden and the gull, if it was the same one, flew onto the roof where it complained bitterly.

As she was descending the rock, very slowly and carefully, a massive pain gripped her, forcing her tongue between her teeth and making her hit her head against the rough surface. She slid slowly down the rock face, nails tearing at the moss and lichen until she came to rest, head pillowed on the clump of sea grass at the bottom. For an instant she heard the thin mewling cry of a baby. Her baby and he needed her.

She tried to struggle out of the web of sleep, as she had so often done when children cried in the night, groping through the darkness and fighting the desire for unconsciousness, but this time the blackness claimed her inexorably.

The wailing gull wheeled high above the limp body stretched at the foot of the rock, its arms stretched out as if ready to receive and hold something, or someone.

What
Great Big
Teeth You've Got

Mary Donovan

THE NUNS said that Kathleen was brainy, and, fair enough, she always walked through her exams, but Mrs. Mahony knew that her Kathleen wasn't, couldn't possibly be the full shilling. A girl that couldn't go down for a message without leaving her gloves behind? A girl that came near to being knocked down crossing the road in Coolbawn, where even the hens and ducks could cross. Of course, Kathleen would take it into her head to cross over just when Jim Clancy was tearing off to his greyhound meeting, and she didn't see Jim because, as usual, her head was stuck in a book. Only for the grace of God and Jim's brakes — Mrs. Mahony could hear the screech still. What was worse, though Mrs. Mahony lost no chance to remind her daughter of how near she'd come to death, Kathleen seemed no more worried about it than a new-born babe would be.

''Twas probably all that studying that had turned her brain.' But this was the girl who in three weeks' time was due to start life in Dublin.

'Jack', said Mrs. Mahony, when Kathleen had gone to bed, 'I was talking to Annie today, and her two girls have a lovely flat somewhere near the college. Two streets away, she said.

85

'Twould be ideal if Kathleen moved in with them. They're two sensible girls who'd mind their belongings and lock and bolt the door at night.'

Jim gave his wife the usual guff about the girl being well able to look after herself when she got the chance but the following Sunday he drove to Dublin and secured his daughter a place in a hostel attached to a convent, within walking distance of the college.

So, Kathleen found herself in a big playground called Dublin where there were new streets to walk in every day, libraries where there were manuscripts and old newspapers and you were allowed take them down and read them, a college players' club of which, wonder of wonders, she was allowed to become a member, where she could watch Gareth turning them into the Christmas Revue.

Every day, she found another wonder, but no dangers. And give her her due, she tried her best to find some dangers. Her father had warned her to keep her eyes peeled for dangers and she felt that she owed it to him to accept the warning. So at first she would concentrate very hard every time she used an escalator, or stairs on a bus, and look hard at the people around her, wondering could they be muggers or bank robbers. But so many of the people she met were so friendly — talking with her, picking up things she'd dropped, that she soon realised that her father was mistaken. It was a bit of a blow — she'd suspected for a long time that her mother's ideas were a bit foolish but she'd always had great faith in her father.

One night in November she went to a session in Thomas Street and got a bit high on the music. Walking home she liked the fact that there were people still walking out at this hour. She liked the fact that she was doing something she wouldn't be allowed to at home. She liked the old signs on the shops and the pubs which looked as if strangers never went into them. She liked the posters plastered everywhere — reminded her of Seamus who brought home the pictures he drew at school and stuck them up in his bedroom. She liked the way the moon shone right down into the street.

Then she came across an arch. It seemed to be a fine arch

and she stood looking up at it. Suddenly something bumped against her and said 'Sardy'.

She turned round and saw a young man. His face looked yellow and tired with the street lamp glaring on it. He was looking at her uncertainly. She smiled at him and said 'It was my fault – I was looking at the arch'.

He flicked his eyes over the arch and couldn't find anything to keep them there.

'You were looking at the arch?'

'Yes. I love looking at arches.'

He'd never come across one with that line of chat before.

'You seem to be on your own?'

'Yes, I've been to the session in the hall down there.'

'On your own.'

'Oh, yes.'

'And you're not afraid?'

'Afraid?'

'Afraid to be walking out with no guard nor nothing.'

'Oh, no. There weren't any guards where I grew up either.'

Ah, a culchie. But surely they weren't as green as all that?

'You're not afraid of being mugged or anything?'

Kathleen couldn't help laughing.

'My mother is always going on about fellows in Dublin who lie in wait for girls and –' she realised that what she was saying must be embarrassing, maybe hurtful to the poor fellow so she started gabbling about her mother's views on the Dublin traffic. 'I've survived in Dublin a whole month now and she can't understand it.'

'Do you mind if I walk along with you?'

'Sure – I mean I don't mind.'

So they walked on, she opening her eyes to the strange buildings, he looking at the strange girl.

'I'm Jimmy.'

'I'm Kathleen.'

Kathleen – real culchie name alright.

'Kathleen – real nice name. Gentle. Look, Kathleen, do you always carry your purse like that?'

Kathleen pushed down the purse, closed the shoulder-bag and clapped her hand over it as her mother had taught her. 'I know, it's foolish, but I keep forgetting. Still, I don't think I've had anything stolen on me so far.'

'Think?'

'Hmm? Oh, well, you see, I never know how much I had going out in the first place, so — . But I don't think I've met any thieves.'

He thought for a minute and then he said 'Kathleen?'

'Jimmy?'

'When you were at school, did people say that you were backward?'

Kathleen started to giggle. 'My mother used always say that I had no more sense than a child of six.' After a while she said, 'My father never said it in so many words, but I think he thinks I'm a bit wanting too. The day he brought me up here, he showed me how to catch a bus and how to read the timetable. Then he took me into the GPO and showed me three times how to work the 'phone box. The third time he said we'd get through to some pal of his in Dublin, but we were wasting our time because it was an overseas box. You see, we don't have overseas callboxes or dial telephones at home — everything goes through the operator.

'He took me into Wynn's for lunch and told me that I'd had a very sheltered life and that there were three things I was not to do — get involved with strangers, get on a bus that had no number and walk along the quays, or anywhere else, after dark. He bought me a key-ring that clipped onto my watch. Then we studied the bus timetable again and caught a bus going to the hostel and he had a long chat with one of the nuns . . .' she paused.

'You're in school here with the nuns?'

'Oh, no, not in school — I'm finished with that. I'm seventeen.'

'You're not!' He knew she was having him there — by seventeen, all girls had grown hard mouths and hidden themselves behind make-up.

'I am. The nuns have a hostel and I'm staying there for a year instead of in a flat.'

This was all a bit weird, but she was a nice looking piece.

'Kathleen, would you like a drink? I know a pub along here where they'd serve us no bother.'

'Drink? Oh, no thanks, I don't drink.'

'Given it up?'

'No, I never took it up at all.'

'You're joking me.'

'No.'

'You've never drank at all?'

Deciding she'd like to match his humorous tone, Kathleen asked him if all the girls he knew were great drinkers, and she wondered how he could think up such vivid stories. He talked about the girl who, unknown to anyone else, had been putting aspirins in her vodka 'rigid she was, like a bottle-brush', she fell backwards off the barstool and couldn't be woken up for eight hours, and about girls who drank brandy and climbed the cinema roof to escape the wicked motor cars. At home, she'd never met such a skilled talker. Neither, at home, were there midnight streets where your step sounded as distinctly as in a room, where the light made the buildings look as if they were saying 'Come on over and look at me'.

She stepped across the road to see more clearly the wood-work on a shopfront. Jimmy couldn't work out what she was doing, then he noticed all the cigarettes in the window.

'It would madden you all right.'

'What, Jimmy?'

'All them cigarettes. Have a smoke?' He pulled out a battered packet containing three cigarettes.

'Oh, no thank you, I don't smoke.'

He lit one himself. 'Yeah. All them hundreds of cigarettes and all I've left is a lousy two.'

'Tee-hee! You remind me of my father. He used to smoke. He'd get fierce edgy when the cigarettes were running out. He's a real mild man usually but I think he'd nearly have robbed a shop for cigarettes.

'This place'd be easy to rob' Jimmy said, going over to the grid and handling it as if he meant to go to work on it.

'Matter of fact, it was done last week — the old fella who

owns it is too mean to buy a proper what-you-call-it.'

'Grid?'

'Yeh. D'you see here? All it needs is a few turns of a screw-driver, a bit of pressure and there you are. A pity I haven't my screwdriver on me, I'd show you.'

'What about the window?'

'No bother — bash it in with a stone. Or tie a rag round your fist.'

'Like in the films?'

'You don't believe me? I'm telling you, that's how it's done.'

'But wouldn't the noise bring the cops?'

'Cops? Jaysus, do you think any cop'd come here? There hasn't been a cop in these parts since one of them got his head smashed in tor him.'

'Ugh.' She preferred his conversation without the lurid bits.

'Tell me, Kathleen, what would you do if you heard a brick going in a window?'

She said nothing for a while. 'I — well — I've never heard a brick going through a window — maybe I'm a bit deaf or something.' She stopped awhile.

'But if I did — well — I like to think that I'd get up and — challenge the robber.'

'Kathleen, you know what? You're not dumb — you're mad.'

Glass crashed. Kathleen's mouth went dry. She whispered 'I'd better go and see what it is' and she forced her legs, one before the other across the street.

Jimmy came after her. 'It's only a wino, that guy over there.'

Kathleen walked closer to the holed window and worked herself up to look at the man who'd thrown the bottle. He was slight, fragile-looking. His clothes might have been worn for several years by several differently shaped men. He had a young face, a face you might see in a holy picture, gentle and intense at the same time. He said 'Please help me.' He said it in the way a child would who'd been told to put expression into a poem. His eyes tried to winch her in.

'Help?' she said. She didn't know what else to say, but she desperately wanted to help him.

'No money — look — stolen — someone stole it on me — need money — buy wine — need some wine.' The eyes pulled and pulled.

'Come on Kathleen,' Jimmy said and the wino backed away.

Kathleen said 'He's asking for help.' She couldn't say 'I'm afraid to turn away from him' because she hadn't realised this long enough to put it into words. She was on a tightrope — she could jump down on the side of ignoring him, in which case she might be refusing a man in need. If she jumped down on the other side, where might she end up?

'He might be sick,' she said. 'He might need to be helped home.'

'Home? Guys like him have no home. He sleeps wherever he falls down.'

Kathleen turned to the wino and asked him where he lived. He looked at her, it seemed, for several minutes and he seemed to spin around. He shambled off to a railing and lay against it.

A wave of perspiration broke through Kathleen's skin. She looked round and her eye landed on a telephone box. The police would know what to do. It wasn't until she'd listened for the dial tone and heard nothing that she realised why she'd never get through.

'Guts ripped out?' Jimmy asked.

'Yes.'

She found three boxes in that condition, then she said 'Jimmy, I'm going to the Pearse Street station.' She started to run, it seemed very important to run. She didn't stop running until she came to the station. Two Gardaí tight-skinned under the fluorescent light, listened to her. They didn't seem to be all that worried about the wino, or the window, but they promised to send round a squad car. They got her to fill in a lot of spaces on a form. 'St. Jude's Hostel? Two turns to the left?'

She thought it out and said yes.

'Garda Hennessy'll take you home in the squad car.'

'There's no need, thanks, I'll be okay.'

She had to say this, she couldn't allow herself to think that she might be terrified. But when they insisted, she allowed herself to be driven.

She had her key ready before the squad car stopped. Very quickly, she opened the door and closed it behind her. Walking up the stairs, she passed someone, someone whose eyes were big and attracting. Kathleen fled to her room and locked the door.

En Famille

Rita F. Kelly

CATHERINE turned from her own image in the window. Stiff, yet shaken, the continual clatter, carriage off carriage, bone within socket, even the breast shook in its shaping cup. Something primitive in the constant trundle. A hand reached up to the luggage-rack, it was reduplicated in the window, a suitcase slipped down at an angle, can't be far off, she tensed herself, prepared her ears, knowing the steel bridge five hundred yards before the station. The thundering rattle of steel, every bolt shocked into its part in the shattering crescendo.

Lights, always dim at railway stations, she stepped out into a sprinkle of rain, steam hissing from the heating system, shreds of voices, smell of oil, somewhere at her back the engine idling, yet with a mechanical insistence to jerk ahead, pull its load to the next stop. The air is pierced, a jerk, a door banged shut, another, the dull resounding thud. Light flickers across her face, quicker and quicker, figures walk back against the motion, faces, limbs, luggage coming and gone. Finally the black hole in the air, drawing and repulsing as if the eyes were struck. Things settle themselves, a footbridge, the further platform, railings, lights repeating themselves in damp surfaces. Man in the signal-box pulling and twisting, contorting himself about the huge wheel while below ever so slowly the gates creak back, cars move again before the gates clash to, shutting off the tracks, the man in the box straightens himself, adjusts his cap.

'Taxi, miss?'

'No thank you, I . . .'

But the taximan was already taking suitcases from a family party and ushering them towards the exit. One of the smaller children stumbled and cried before falling. The fatigue and bother of travelling, well past its bedtime and all the strange excitement drained out of the day. The father picked it up, it leaned on his shoulder, his long step, up and down, the child's hat bobbing away into the distance . . .

'Catherine! Over here!' Yes, it is her name, called sharply out of the murk and drizzle. James of course, his usual hurry, she imagined him being incited, dragged away from his stereo or a book, she felt her coming a mistake, she had been too dazed to object strongly enough. Barbara was so persuasive at a distance. He was taking her bag, still not accustomed to him as a brother-in-law, at once related and alien. He held her to his rough dufflecoat. Always that awkward hug, must have discovered somewhere that kissing is unhygienic, or else the propensity had atrophied because Barbara does not approve. Leading the way to the car he interrupted his flow of trite remarks to wish people good evening, something too determined about the tone he adopted, they could scarcely be more than acquaintances, he seemed anxious to justify his being seen at the station with an unknown woman. And Catherine was being invited to note that the man with the trilby hat was the town's operatic tenor, his wife, president of the Ladies' Golf Committee.

At the car she stood aloof waiting for James to unlock the anti-theft device, the boot, the passenger door. She knew that a comment was expected from her on the new model, but she took a spiteful pleasure in letting him search for it.

'Just got the numberplates on yesterday. Continental, you

know, way ahead on suspension. Overhead camshaft, low air resistance, real smooth, can't you notice the difference?'

'But I thought you felt the Japanese model to be away ahead on everything.'

'Well, Barbara felt they were becoming too common, besides it was a bit cramped you know, very little leg-room. No harm in having a bit of luxury.

The wipers swished before them. A long suburban road, houses well back, lights placed in an alternate pattern, parked cars on both sides. Catherine leaned forward to wipe the condensation from the glass with her gloved hand.

'I'd prefer if you didn't, it leaves a smear, besides the blower will clear it in a minute.'

'I see. Forgive me, I'm so unacquainted with the technical advances.'

She stared at the panel of green dials, a frozen light, easy on the eyes perhaps, yet could all those clocks and dials be necessary, were they just stating the obvious, or was it the intention to create a cockpit interior? A more complicated and overtly technical toy? A red light stopped flashing as James belatedly released the handbrake.

'Barbara would have come with me but didn't dare leave the Infanta. I have a horror of babysitters too – one's own flesh and blood, such a risk nowadays, besides having some youngster poke about the house, know what I mean?'

'Of course, an unavoidable disadvantage.'

'Leaving the child?'

'No, having to apologise for not leaving it.'

Catherine decided to take a grip on her irony, too sharp, too complex, a symptom merely of her nerve-shaken frustration. She settled back in her seat, comfortable after the jolting train. The journey, the city, above all the college, receded, it was as if some other person were involved. Here it was again, the immediacy of James and Barbara, their life blotted out her own, transformed her somehow. The town seemed asleep, the odd pedestrian, the odd dog, a huddle of cars at the hotel. Something negative, something static, perhaps she could get away from herself in this atmosphere, if only she could sustain the attack of domesticity, and the inundation of fashionable pseudotheories, so stupidly *simplistes* —

'Paternal instinct is quite a phenomenon.'

'Really?'

'Yes. I don't think it's quite understood, I mean I instinctively wake up and jump out of bed before I have thoroughly registered the fact that Niamh is whimpering.'

'I should think it's because Barbara has you so well trained.'

'But I have a strange feeling, bang on, when she needs a nappy change, very odd . . .'

'Surely it doesn't take an extraordinary instinct to discover that?'

'Have you read Cohen on paternal instinct?'

'Sorry, I'm afraid teacher training at present is learning to avoid the detritus of the pseudosciences.'

'But this is really interesting, remind me to show it to you.'

'The paternal instinct?'

'Seems I have been misled. You don't sound in the least out of sorts.'

'Does one have to sound it?'

'All this won't prevent you taking your diploma, I hope? It would be such a terrible waste.'

'It won't — though it is difficult to decide what is waste in the context.'

'You know what I mean, things have become so competitive, it's important to have something to show. You must finish at the training college. Nothing wrong with teaching, good money, of course I have no experience of the primary section, but I feel that they work out better than we do, less pressure, easier to handle the younger ones.'

He continued his monologue until he brought the car to a halt in the driveway. The confined sense, the press of the neighbouring facades, as if he might have parked at someone else's front. She stepped out, felt her foot sink in soft earth, flower border, daffodils, whether the car was too big or the driveway specification too meagre, there was nowhere else to step. She concealed her *faux pas* as James busily locked the car doors, opened the front door, the garage and the boot. She may find her own way in, Barbara will be in the kitchen.

She finds herself moving cautiously along the hallway, the narrowness, the conventional furnishings, telephone, potted creeper, coatstand, an openwork stairway, probably saves material, and a mirror never intended to reflect anything because of its impossible angle. A barometer in under the stairs, it could hardly be read without a bump on the head. She lingers, alone with herself again. If only Barbara would appear or call, she must have heard the door open. She feels an intruder, pushing against an unwelcome, stealing into the house. Again, that confusion, the indecision, too late to turn back, she might be discovered loitering if Barbara suddenly appeared. In shoe shops, department stores, at railway stations, penetrating to the ladies' room in hotels, confusion, hesitation. She tries to overcome the feeling, taps at the kitchen door. No response. The feeling returns much stronger, yet she turns the handle and enters. Nothing. A smell of cooking. Then Barbara came from the outer kitchen with an armful of clothes.

'Oh you've come. Train late? Just finishing the ironing. Would you stir the soup, I must run upstairs with this load.'

Catherine removed her gloves and left her handbag on a chair, stepped on a plastic duck which uttered a complaining squeak. She found the soup and a spoon. Glancing about she noticed the newness of things, pretty curtains, ingredients in jars and bottles clearly marked, little zigzag shelves for spices and flavourings, the sink a melée of potato-skins, tea-leaves and dirty dishes. Two small shoes and stockings on the floor, she bent to pick them up, James entered behind her.

'Did no one take your coat? Where's Barbara?'

'I'm here. She knows well where to leave her coat. Dinner in a few minutes. James, why don't you set the fire in the sittingroom.'

He changed into slippers and began to pass back and forth with a coalscuttle. Something about the slippers disconcerted Catherine, repulsed her. Barbara gave the impression of being absorbed with the dinner preparations, yet in control.

'Want a drink, Kate? I can't touch it you know, damn

all the sacrifices I make for those kids, I'm sure you were surprised when you heard I was pregnant again, well they're nicely spaced anyway. Leave those, sit down, rest yourself. I'm glad you've come, at least a new face, someone to talk to. Nothing strange I suppose? Has Mam been moaning to you too, I nearly ate her on the 'phone the other night, what the hell is wrong with her, she was never as well off, as if I didn't have enough to worry about, but she wouldn't say she'd come over and stay for a while, give me a break, I get so tired, especially in the afternoon and Niamh is a handful, very difficult child. I'd better run up again, lately she has started to climb out of her cot . . . Would you? If she makes strange call me, she can be such a little bitch.'

Catherine found the room, its dim light, probably afraid of the dark. Niamh was stretched fast asleep, the little fingers wrapt round the rag doll. Catherine is amused, rather flattered, that the doll she made for her should be so particularly accepted. The breathing is somewhat heavy, the mouth partially open. Stray strands of hair glisten on the pillow. She kneels, watching. She ought to steal away, if the child wakens she is bound to be upset. But there is something gripping about the child, lost in her own little dream, overcome by the day's round, the meals, the sounds, the stumbles, the daylit places at once known intimately and terribly unknown. Yet she is Barbara's child, a stranger really, imbibing the tone, having the common characteristics painted within. Dyed in the genes, perhaps. Too easy to be attracted by the sleeping child, the sentimental pose, too easy to forget the reality, the complaining plastic duck, one's own inadvertance. And Catherine drew away from the cot, conquering the wish to touch the delicate skin, the small lips protruding.

'Well, was she alright?'

'Sound asleep.'

'That's odd, normally the little devil has to be begged to lie down. Would you call James, he's probably stuck in a book, tell him it's on the table.'

Barbara made an effort at acting the gracious hostess, presiding over her dinner-service, silver and cut glass. Wedding presents most likely, brought out on special occasions, perhaps when some of James's colleagues came to dinner, otherwise there can't have been many occasions. But Catherine felt, as with the pretty curtains and the labelled jars, a certain playing at haus frau, grown-up babyhouse, which a normal sane remark might shatter. Like weighing out clay and pretending it was sugar, or mixing mud in a paint-tin and pretending it was sweetcake. If someone, tired of the game of finding themselves outside the circle of make-believe, remarked on the mud, everything would stop suddenly, then pouting, tears, and a smashing of jam-jars on stone.

James almost shattered the effect at times, obviously he needed further practice, but a glance from Barbara saved the moment. Catherine played her part, found pertinent comments, asked about preparations and recipes, admired the design of the cut-glass bowls. It was an attempt at being amiable, at acknowledging the trouble Barbara had so obviously taken. Yet a hug or even a warm handshake would have meant so much, but it would have caused Barbara greater effort.

Conversation fluctuated about the particular, the home, the car, the child existing and the child expected. Catherine helped with the coffee, which was to be served in the sitting-room, washing up was abandoned until the morning. Barbara decided that they didn't want to watch the news, James eventually agreed and replenished the fire.

There was some lack of comfort in the room despite the large velvet-covered suite and the wall-length velvet curtains. Television and stereo equipment dominating, a Van Gogh print, an antique writing-desk, a shelf of sitting-room books, children's encyclopedias, the rest loud, mixed, only moved when dusting. Catherine had never experienced the room in such a way before. The encyclopedias especially irritated her, as if they were part of the equipment needed for having children, like prams and soothers, some responsibility had been fulfilled, the intellectual life of the child had not been forgotten. Very likely the house next door repeats the pattern, it is no doubt repeated along the Drive, a change of colour perhaps, some slight shift of emphasis, a different set of discs or encyclopedias, but the same mental and material specifications.

James tiring of the domestic preoccupations brought the conversation round to evolution, some recent reading, Darwin in the Galapagos Islands, long-legged tortoises, iguanas, Barbara cocked an eye and stressed her breathing. Yet he continued. Catherine found the scraps of information mildly interesting but out of context, such an unimaginative attempt at conversation, he must have known he was boring Barbara who reached the limits of her endurance as the flightless cormorants raised their heads.

'James, for Christ's sake give us a break. It's all very interesting I'm sure, but it's not my idea of a relaxed conversation, and I'm sure Catherine is bored stiff, if she's not I am. Surely you can keep that kind of stuff for your darling Leaving Certs.'

Catherine shifted in her chair. Basically Barbara was correct, but the intolerance of it, the unkindness, while her own topics of conversations were so penetratingly banal. She had grown sharper in tone and in feature, even the eyes were too obvious, too protruberant. But James accepted the cut with a feeble effort at humour. Adaption to environment? Survival of the fittest? Catherine tried to manoeuvre a safe shift, but nothing seemed quite safe in this atmosphere. However . . .

'Niamh has got big since I saw her last.'

'I'll soon have opposition. Even as it is . . .'

'And very intelligent, you'd hardly believe. Of course Barbara tried to claim responsibility for that.'

'Without much hope I should think? Catherine felt her tone grow bright and artificial, echo of college conversations, pretending an interest.'

'Naturally. He is such a clever father. All I seem to have contributed is her cranky moods.'

'Her IQ must be way up. You see, Catherine, children have an open pipeline to the seat of creativity, it must be kept open, all in the right hemisphere of the brain, you understand functional psychology, very important, and the toys nowadays are so creative, schematized to widen the horizons.'

'James is right for once. He brought her this fantastic thing from London — the school trip to Stratford — you should see it, little round things all different colours and sizes, multi-dimensional, and they all fit into each other in the most striking patterns.'

'It even took me a few hours to get the hang of it myself.'

'But Kate, I could have strangled her. David and Laura were here too, remember James, she took one look at it, put on a puss and said, "I don't like it," and went off with that bloody awful rag doll.'

'But Catherine sent her that doll — '

'Oh yes, very nice and all that, but it has got so scruffy.'

'Sorry about that . . .' She flushed, sat still, palms pressed to her knees.

'But when I think of what he paid for it, I mean it's intolerable, God, when we were kids . . .'

'Oh it's not the money, Barbara, for goodness sake.'

'Your multidimensional fresh from London is meant to find the pipeline to the child's left hemisphere, one supposes. Seat of logic, isn't it?' Her lips were in prim control of the sarcasm, inwardly seething. 'But logic, I daresay, is a bad word in the pedagogical junk biz?'

Brother-in-law wasn't really listening, he missed the shaft maliciously aimed at him.

'Forgive me, ladies, I've got some work to prepare. I know it must sound awfully old-fashioned, but with the lot I have I've got to keep abreast.'

'H'm, in order to keep abreast of them I know what I'd do!'

He left. Perhaps he did have some work to do, but she found the emphasised conscientiousness distasteful. The dedicated professional act. Barbara poked the fire, leaned back in her armchair, kicked a stool under her feet. She seemed to expand her stomach, stressing the pregnancy, the acme of feminine ethos. So aware, the supine position, so much like a pale heroine on a chaise longue, the arm at a pathetic angle and some sal volatile to hand. Something shamelessly typical about the posture, an act that was no act but a choking arche-type, now that the male, that necessary irritant, had been driven from the scene.

'Did you hear all that crap about the school, makes me sick. He's more concerned about them than he is about me.'

'You're not inclined to over-react are you?'

'So I'm over-reacting am I? Easy for you, you don't know what it's like.'

'But surely it can't be that bad, perhaps you're just going through a patch of ill-humour, being pregnant is a strain.'

'Oh if you mean that I hadn't wished it.'

'Surely some of the methods are dependable?'

'It's not that, Kate, you see I must consider myself to be lucky to be pregnant at all.'

'You can't mean . . .'

'We sleep together, as yet anyway, but I might as well not be there. Oh I read the books.'

'Tried the aphrodisiacs I suppose?'

'The lot, from wheatgerm to shock tactics. Then it finally dawned on me. That school, all those girls, even the nuns, it does something to them, I mean it's bound to, siphons off the sexual energy, then he comes home absolutely spent.'

'But the job is rather demanding. I imagine you would feel rather spent yourself.'

'I know all that, but this is something extra, now if he were teaching in a boys' school.'

'Then you might have other problems.'

'No, Kate, I'm really convinced, you see during the holidays it's quite different. What man could spend his time among a crowd of girls, mostly nubile, and not be affected, you know what they're like.'

'Yes, but you would have expected the opposite effect wouldn't you?'

'All I'm saying is that it's not healthy.'

'I suppose Origen would agree with you.'

'Please, if that's some authority on educational theory, I don't want to know.'

'A very practical man when it came to the instruction of

young women. A doctor of the Church. Had himself castrated to avoid temptation. Still, I think you may be simplifying the situation.'

'But I've noticed things, not just once or twice, I still do the washing round here.'

'Alright, Barbara, let's not be crude. Mind if I go to bed now? I'm mentally drained, must be the journey.'

'Sure, why not. I think I might lie on in the morning. Help yourself, Niamh will be running about of course, and James has an early start.'

'Goodnight.'

'My good nights are over for another few months.'

In bed, Catherine tried to relax but jerked awake each time she was on the point of sinking into sleep. Barbara came up, she could hear her mutterings from the master-bedroom as they liked to call it, water, walking, wardrobe doors. Privacy: laths and a skin of plaster. Even from the house next door she heard rumblings, a telephone bell, steps on stairs. Living within earshot of the neighbour. Copulation in one house probably sets up a chain-reaction along the Drive, Barbara's an end house, she loses half the stimulation. A toilet is flushed next door, a door bangs, silence. Her book absorbs the restless churning of her mind for two hours or more, still no sleep. She gets up, draws aside the curtain, faces her dim self and a small lit window in the distance. She switches off her lamp and the further houses shape themselves against a diffused light in the sky, a moon somewhere, the gardens form into dark rectangles between cold walls of concrete. The window rattles in a gust of wind, a clothesline in the next garden bangs off its steel post, metallic sound empty of meaning.

In bed again she relives the thud and rattle of the train. Nerves and wires vibrating. Mechanized universe, mechanized mind. The college course grinding through its gears, the small minds, myriads of them, living blobs of imagination, crushed and ironed out in the mechanism. Not sleep really, but strangled in the recurring nightmare.

April, the rustle and scream of birds in morning light. The little face had come close to the edge of her pillow. Doll and hands up tight under the chin, a face oddly shrunk and wizened. Eyes half shut, colourless, lids creased wrinkling the little ancient face from which the eyes squinted at her, in cunning, in curiosity, or in something older than either of them, complicity. Gone silently, she heard the awkward yet determined clop of bare feet down the stairs. Cups and cutlery sounded against each other from the kitchen.

New Country

Gabrielle Warnock

THE HOUSE had been their pride. Their emblem of
continuity, eternity. Sarah could vividly recall the afternoon
on which they had discovered the ruin. The boreen had
enticed first. A green, quiet tunnel, an entrance to the stone
scaled mountain. Martin, in his goose green jersey, his thinning
corduroy jeans, had faded into the lane, and his boots which
had chinked along the edge of the road went dead on moss.
The cessation of that sound had been so quietening, Sarah
could almost have bent to kiss the soft moss. Even his voice,
calling back to her had been muffled, the excitement contained.

'Sarah, love, there's the wall of a house up here.'

And sure enough, there was. The passage of the boreen was
stoppered by a tall, lichen crusted wall. Once, the boreen had
made a right-angled turn at the wall. Now, it disintegrated to
a cattle wide path of trampled mud and waves of side scratch-
ing brambles. Martin was waiting there for her, holding back
barbed lengths of brambles that she might pass safely through.

'Easy now Sarah, mind you don't catch on those thorns.'

As she had passed by him, she had sensed him wanting to

touch her, and had been glad that his hands were trapped by chivalry. It was she who had discovered that there was a second, third and fourth wall.

'Martin,' she had said. 'It's complete.'

And her eyes had actually met his. And for a moment, her hand had trembled, as though it might have moved towards . . . but no. Still, Martin had noticed, and had smiled his huge, warm smile. Oh, but luck was with them. The lintels, the gables, the chimney breast were all intact. No trees grew inside the door. Only the brambles had pushed through the empty windows, had drooped listlessly down to the floor, nuzzled their tips into the warmer earth, and then had sent up new, invigorated shoots. Sarah had seen Martin looking at those brambles, and she had known he was thinking that in such a house, he and she might be reborn, like the shoot. And she had resented him for his fanciful thinking, while knowing that the thought had also been hers.

'We'd kill the place. By doing anything,' she had said flatly. 'You couldn't let lorries drive up that boreen with all the rafters and the slates. The slabs for the floor. It'd only be spoilt.'

'Maybe not.' Martin had spoken softly, had gone to the fireplace and had run his hand round the curve of the arch. 'We could buy a bit of a field with it maybe. Grow things. Vegetables and the like. A few hens. Such tranquility.'

She'd seen that he was thinking as much of his writing as of her. She'd thought of not having to hear the children, Timothy and Roseen, laughing and fighting next door.

She had nodded. 'It would be nice to grow vegetables. I like growing things. Let's go outside the house. Take a look around.'

The door faced the mountain. A cold door, but an exhilarating door. A door to explore through. To open it up in the morning, and see, not the sticky leaved escallonia, but that expanse of soil-robbed mountain, and to feel the wind and the rain skinning you. Between the house and the mountain lay a wide band of cultivation where some of the mountain soil had been dropped. The perimeter of each field was protected by a jaw of stones, making wicked walls. If there was the ruin, then there might be a bit of a field in it for them too.

'We'll build ourselves into this. A safe place to be. We'll let the house grow around us, form us.' This time, Martin had nodded as he spoke, and he had put his arm most firmly around Sarah's shoulder, before she had time to move away. 'Won't we, Sarah?'

'We might, Martin.'

A spring sun had eased memories from the earth that day. A nostalgic smell of damp, unfolding leaves. And there had been early celandines hiding down the boreen.

It had obviously been pre-arranged. The old man was so taken aback that someone should want to buy a house abandoned by himself, that he sold to them in a hazy aura of disbelief that anyone should be so half-baked as to take on such a heap of stone. When they might just as well have put up a pre-fab in the same time that it would take them to roof and floor the cottage.

'Well and all, there's no accounting for tastes,' he said as they exchanged deeds. He even parted with some square feet of the adjoining field, to see what sort of fools they might make of themselves with that.

All through that spring and summer, they worked devotedly on the cottage. They brought a tent up to the place, and camped in their tiny vegetable field. Weeks they spent nailing up the rafters, and when they had finished, the house looked beautiful, like the reversed hull of a wrecked ship. It was so beautiful they delayed putting the skin on top of the frame, just so that they could admire it. Their clothes smelled of creosote, and creosote crept in drops along the rafters for days. They were intent on protecting their house so that their house would protect them. After the skin, the lathes, and at last, the slates. Even when the roof was on, and the glass had been puttied into the new teak window frames, they remained in their tent. They didn't want to enter their territory until it was properly prepared, so they laboured over the stone work, pointing it, scrubbing it, laying stone slabs for the floor. Local slabs, with worm traceries indented on the surfaces.

The fourth room they divided in two. A tiny bathroom and a tiny study. Martin led the water from the well into the house, so that they had one temperamentally flushing lavatory, and a bath into which cold, brown water ran.

And between them, a more normal relationship developed. It was difficult to avoid contact spreadeagled out over a roof, terrified of falling off. Perhaps it was less negative than that. Perhaps Sarah found it easier to break out of her pattern of isolation under unusual circumstances. She was able to make the first contacts less noticeable. Without having to imagine the slightly pitiful hopes in Martin's mind. So that almost without effort, they were past that stage, and had become accustomed to touching hands as they passed slates from one to another, exchanged tools. Occasionally, Sarah would touch Martin, on the hand, or on the cheek, and say, 'look,' drawing his attention maybe to a raven soaring above them, or sunlight shining on wet rock. And he would be careful not to catch hold of the hand that touched him, and it might lie there for a few moments, resting on his skin like a butterfly.

Finally there had been the night that they moved into the cottage. They had lit a fire of hazelwood, and two stubby white candles shone to themselves in the niches on either side of the stone arch. In the arc of heat, Sarah and Martin made love. It was an act almost without self-consciousness. Afterwards neither of them could speak of it for fear of disturbing the fragility. It had been the first time in more than a year. Not even in the proximity of the tent.

It was Donal, the old man, who disturbed. A crapulous, drink-infested old man, full of curiosity about Martin and Sarah. Martin described his curiosity as the direct simplicity of the countryside. Sarah thought of it as inquisitiveness.

'He's only trying to place us in his order of things.'

But Sarah thought that the questions stemmed from suspicion, and the desire to be the one to know about them first. And why shouldn't he be suspicious of them? Weren't they different to anyone that he had ever come across? What if they turned out to be bad eggs, hippies or the like? It would be Donal who would get stick from the neighbours, for it would be Donal who had brought them into the place. Martin could understand Donal. He enjoyed talking to the old man, had patience with the questions. It was understandable that Donal should ask Martin why it was that he didn't have a job. It would seem strange that a man should always be around the house. So Martin showed him some of his books, with his name on the covers. After that, Donal had a great respect for Martin, and for a time could scarcely be persuaded to give an opinion on anything, for fear Martin might disagree with him, or worse, laugh at him. He got over that though. It came to be a habit that Donal would walk across the fields from his own bare bungalow on a Friday evening, and would sit in with Sarah and Martin for an hour or so, over a pint. Sarah dreaded the hour. She hated the way Donal would look around the cottage, with avarice gleaming in his eyes. And he'd always say it was well for those with the money. They both knew that Donal had more money than themselves. Martin said it was wistfulness, not avarice, that showed. A sadness that something should have passed from him. Martin reckoned that Donal was happiest in his bungalow, but that when he came down to the cottage, he was haunted with nostalgia for his youth.

'You're soft,' Sarah finally snapped, and Martin said nothing in reply.

But Martin didn't know the fullness of Donal's curiosity. There were aspects to life which Donal discussed with Martin alone. Racing and drinking, for instance. Equally, there were aspects which he would only bring up with Sarah. Subjects which he might have left to his wife, had she not been dead. Since he felt responsibility for the couple, he took it upon himself to question. It was a day in November when he first asked. A warm, dry day, and Sarah was outside, digging at the patch of ground which was to be their vegetable garden.

'You'll strain your innards doing that.'

Sarah grunted as she riddled the earth with her fork. Martin had already done the serious digging, the turning over of the sod. She was just playing with the soil and dreaming really.

'It's not right for women to do that sort of work. It's no wonder you have no family yet.' He was standing a certain distance from her, and his eyes were examining her shape. He was trying to tell if she was pregnant or not. He came closer then, lowered his voice. 'Still, you might be right to carry on the way you do,' he said confidentially. 'My Missus always said the house was unlucky. She never had any children. She blamed it on the house. She was glad to see the back of the place.'

Sarah said nothing, but she pinned her fork into the ground with her foot, wiped her hands on her jeans. His breath smelled of whiskey, and it was only early afternoon.

'Do you like children, ma'am?'

'I have to go, Donal. I must see about the dinner. Will you excuse me?'

She turned away from him, walked back over the plot towards the house. Martin opened the door as she looked, and a gust of smoke blew out of the chimney. Tears were in her eyes. Donal was following her.

'It'd be grand, all the same, to have a few children running round the place.'

It was March now. Perhaps if she had told Martin at the beginning he would have had a word with Donal, just a quiet warning. But at the time, she hadn't been able to bring herself to mention the conversation. She brooded terribly. Martin was engrossed in a book, which meant minimal attention from him, so that she was left alone for long periods of time. There was no one to talk to. Friends who had called so gaily in the summer months, seldom visited in that winter time. Sarah became morbidly introspective, and it was upon Donal that she focussed all her fear. Until, finally, last night, Friday night, she had screamed at him to take himself off, to go from the house. She didn't say it, but she thought he was like an evil eye. And Donal had dropped his glass to the floor, and then had stood, bundling his coat around him, not looking at either of them, and then had half-run to the door. Martin had tried to open the door for him, but Donal had pushed at him with his hand.

'You'd better stay in.' As though Martin might have gone off with him. His voice was tremulous.

The evening had been so quiet when he had gone. The fire had glittered while they talked. Martin always kept his arm around her, but she felt it must be an effort for him. He said Donal had been just about to leave. That no, she hadn't screamed. She had sounded tired, no more. Donal had dropped the glass because he was a fumbling, fuddled old man, and probably she had reminded him of his wife. But why hadn't she told him that Donal was pestering her? Why? Because when she thought about it, he hadn't been pestering. It was only, as Martin had said, the curiosity of an old man. But all the time Martin was talking so sympathetically, Sarah was thinking that he must be despising her, he must be ashamed of her cruelty. When they had gone to bed, Martin had fallen to sleep long before Sarah. That made her feel alienated. The worst was that he had gone when she woke up. He wasn't in the study. He'd eaten nothing. He'd just gone. She knew he hadn't left her, but the ominous knowledge that he was not in the house oppressed her so much that she had to leave. Maybe he hadn't told her where he was going because he was finally so ashamed of her that he no longer cared whether or not she knew.

She walked up through the fields, towards the mountains, to where the dwarfed hazels grew, microscopic woods, primeval, tangled up in ferns. The ferns were huge, protected by the tiny trees, those cunningly leaved trees, pretending to be evergreen under cloaks of ivy. She wanted to sit with her back pressed up to a tree, without thought, until she grew branches and her hair was streamers of ivy. Because Donal was such a diminished ogre, and she was ashamed of herself. If only Martin had thought, or if she could have come straight out with it herself. If either of them had told Donal that she had been barren for twelve years. But instead, she had expected him to know instinctively. Why would he have known? He didn't know that she and Martin had been married so long. Probably he'd thought they were freshly married, the way they went building the cottage so enthusiastically. And he might have noticed how their constraint together had gradually slipped away as they worked, and in a perfectly natural way, he would have begun to expect changes. And then, with his own wife being childless, he might have begun to worry seriously about the house, wonder if there had been something in what his old woman had said about the place being against children. He wasn't to know the indignity of all those tests and how they had kept on and on testing because they could find nothing wrong with either Martin or Sarah. He couldn't know that they had finally been sent to a psychologist who had turned each of them inside out. Sarah, so humiliated herself, had rejected Martin. Until the house had taken over. And then, just at the most fragile moment of all, Donal had come with his piercing, commonplace questions, his crude directness, his simplicity. To have treated him like that, poor old soak.

She might have cried then, but she was tired, with the walk up the hill, and the sleeplessness of the previous night. Instead of crying, she fell asleep with the tree behind her.

When she woke up, Martin was standing over her. Hadn't she found his note on the bed beside her, saying he'd be back at lunchtime? He'd gone off to town, on a special errand, and looking down on the moss, she found six, ridiculous, long-stemmed reddest of roses. Because she was three months pregnant, and fanciful.